"Hi," Holt said after gathering Wiley close again, almost intimate but more for the audience's benefit. He was steady and open, seeming to will Wiley into not freaking totally out and diving off the back of the stage into the river.

Holt tightened his arm when Wiley unconsciously glanced behind them at the appealing thought. His smile was more chagrin than humor, and he closed his eyes and touched Wiley's hairline with the briefest, softest of kisses.

Wiley unexpectedly shivered from that spot all the way to his toes.

Holt pulled back, stood still a breath, and then lifted his microphone.

DREAMSPUN DESIRES

Dear Reader,

Love is the dream. It dazzles us, makes us stronger, and brings us to our knees. Dreamspun Desires tell stories of love featuring your favorite heartwarming heroes, captivating plots, and exotic locations. Stories that make your breath catch and your imagination soar.

In the pages of these wonderful love stories, readers can escape to a world where love conquers all, the tenderness of a first kiss sweeps you away, and your heart pounds at the sight of the one you love.

When you put it all together, you find romance in its truest form.

Love always finds a way.

Elizabeth North

Executive Director
Dreamspinner Press

Elle Brownlee

Say Yes to a Mess

DREAMSPUN
DESIRES

PUBLISHED BY

DREAMSPINNER
PRESS

Published by
DREAMSPINNER PRESS

5032 Capital Circle SW, Suite 2, PMB# 279,
Tallahassee, FL 32305-7886 USA
www.dreamspinnerpress.com

This is a work of fiction. Names, characters, places, and incidents either
are the product of author imagination or are used fictitiously, and any
resemblance to actual persons, living or dead, business establishments,
events, or locales is entirely coincidental.

Say Yes to a Mess
© 2020 Elle Brownlee

Cover Art
© 2020 L.C. Chase
http://www.lcchase.com
Cover content is for illustrative purposes only and any person depicted
on the cover is a model.

Paperback ISBN: 978-1-64108-231-0
Digital ISBN: 978-1-64405-561-8
Library of Congress Control Number: 2020942866
Paperback published November 2020
v. 1.0

Printed in the United States of America

ELLE BROWNLEE always followed her creative, adventuring spirit. Growing up she loved reading, watching Westerns, and taking long hikes, where she'd craft miniature worlds with moss and rocks while making up stories of what happened there. As an adult, not a lot has changed. She still loves all these things—which makes being a writer such a joy. She also loves rainy days in autumn, National Parks, birding and quilting and stickers, and the perfect cup of tea.

Elle currently juggles plenty of travel, working to make the world a better place, and writing. She's so thankful to be able to share her work with a growing audience, and especially grateful to have you reading along.

Website: www.ellebrownlee.com/index.html
Facebook: www.facebook.com/elle.brownlee
Twitter: @ellebrownlee
Email: brownlee.elle@gmail.com

By Elle Brownlee

DREAMSPUN DESIRES
Two for Trust
Say Yes to a Mess
COAST GUARD RESCUE
Staggered Cove Station

Published by **DREAMSPINNER PRESS**
www.dreamspinnerpress.com

For Tere. You were right.

OH, *I Do!*

Okay all you superfan (Team Kit!) Kittens and (Team Holt!) Holsters—and the rest of you lurkers reading out there—what do we think this big doozy of an announcement the Leydon brothers have been teasing for ages is about?

As we're painfully aware here at OID, *Marry Me!* is in its fifth season, and no matter how many online polls we brigade and hashtags we make trend, it's on the bubble for renewal. How the best, most charming show with the best, most charming gents making wedding dreams come true could be in trouble, while those insufferable house-hunting couples are rolling strong into their gazillionth season, I'll never understand.

Anyway! I'm thinking the big announcement is to goose ratings and interest. I mean, of course it is. But it also seems like there's more going on.

Kit was recently on that super cozy vacay with his honey in Maui!

Kit let slip the big announcement will be made live in his hometown of Odalia!

Kit said we'd never guess, but I'm about to make a guess.

Someone—and I don't mean a very special guest star—is getting married.

I try not to give too much allegiance to one brother over the other, and yes, Holt is always super yummy with his tool belt and know-how, but we're friends (frenemies) here, so let's be real: how much would I lo-o-o-ve to see Kit finally get some magic of his own? So much.

Whatever happens, it promises to be amazing.

As always: Claws out and drills drawn, let's get into it in the comments!

Chapter One

"WHAT are we doing? What am I doing?" Wiley stopped abruptly and turned around. "I can't."

"Wiley, don't you dare." Carla's short legs kept brisk pace directly behind him. She levered onto her toes and pushed on his shoulders to turn him back the other direction. "You always say no. It doesn't matter what, you start with no. You don't get to no your way out of this."

"We live in a small town with three streetlights, two greasy-spoon diners, and zero dating options. Saying no is a survival strategy."

Carla scoffed. "There's things. Things here you could not say no to."

"Name one." Wiley glared at her over his shoulder. "Aside from getting out of here for a while."

She was unmoved. "A list is unimportant. Also, we're going so you can see Kit in person after all these years so, hah. There's a huge one."

The reality of that hit Wiley in the chest at the same time as a huge well of apprehension.

"This is so not a good idea. Maybe I should take that big trip to anywhere I've talked about—" He checked his watch. "—in five minutes."

"No, you can't say no again. And running away to a trip you've put off for two years isn't a pass." Carla punched his arm. "This is your Year of Yes! Remember?"

He considered fighting it. He could roll a reverse and break into a run—Carla was good in the sprint, kind of like an adorable rhino, but she had nothing on his stamina. He'd be home and fortified, and it'd take the rest of the day for her to try and pry him loose. He could actually book a trip—whatever was the cheapest flight to somewhere with an ocean and hot temps and one museum—and go. Not for good, necessarily, but to leave. To get the change of pace and scenery he'd pined for since… too long.

She dug a knuckle into the small of his back, and he started to shrug it off, but her frazzled, desperate sigh was what got to him.

"It's June and I haven't said yes to anything. Which, I'll note, has worked great for me so far."

"Uh, my point exactly. The Year of Yes starts here and now." She huffed and began to push, propelling them both forward. "What we're doing is fine, and yes, you can. For the millionth time already. Also, there's free food."

"That isn't a good enough reason for humiliation."

"Who says you have to be humiliated? Don't plan for this to be awful. You know I hate your self-fulfilling prophecies."

"Only because they come true so often and you're left having to talk me down from the ledge with pints of ice cream and our shared *Persuasion* DVD."

"If you didn't like only the super expensive brand best and didn't always lose the DVD under the sofa or in the laundry or putting it in the cabinet when you got crackers, I wouldn't mind so much." Carla lessened the pressure but kept them moving. "We can go do this and have fun and nothing bad has to happen. Nothing good has to happen either. It can be neutral, something different and of passing interest to do, nothing more."

Wiley made a low noise of complaint and uncertainty.

"Besides...."

He waited but she didn't elaborate, so he reached back and hooked an arm in Carla's, dragging her forward to walk alongside him. "I'm not gonna bail," he promised and tightened the link of their elbows. "Besides what?"

"I just... I want you to have fun. You need to have some fun. You need to get out and have fun."

Carla rarely got serious, but that was her serious voice, and it gave Wiley pause.

"I get out." Wiley's protest was weak. "I have fun," he added, even weaker.

Carla grumbled but didn't mention all the ways they both knew he did neither.

"If you get flustered, remember we're here professionally. That's a good cover."

"What?" Wiley pulled up from his musings.

"A cover, in case seeing Kit makes you blush twenty shades of *oh-my-god-he-looked-at-me* and nearly pass out."

"Please. Why would I pass out? Why would I even blush?"

Carla slowed until Wiley was the one tugging them down the block. Refusing to acknowledge what she was talking about.

"Hmm, let's see. Wait, I know—only that Kit Leydon is your lifetime forever crush, and your arm is like Richard the Third-level huge from hauling around the ginormous torch you've carried for him ever since you two collided next to the jungle gym in third grade."

"We collided next to the slides. And wow, deep-cut historical reference, there. I'm impressed." Wiley sidestepped her very on-point point. "But it's a bit of an exaggeration—I'm very nicely symmetrical from all the running I make you do, thank you."

"Sure, sure. One look in Kit's sparkling cerulean pools and it took you an hour to remember your name. In third grade." Carla glanced at Wiley with narrowed eyes. "Hah, you're blushing already."

Wiley definitely was. He couldn't ignore the heat that rose from his chest to spread down his arms and up his face at the very thought of Kit. But he could get it under control by the time they arrived, same as the butterflies that had surged to life in his belly. At least he could blame it all on the powerwalking they'd done to get from the bakery to the park.

"Look—there's the *Marry Me!* bus. Oh my gosh, it's somehow more tacky in person than it looks on the show. I guess that means they're here and this is happening." Carla pointed at it, as if he could miss it, dominating the quaint cobblestone road alongside the park, gleaming in the sunshine. She checked her watch and increased their pace.

"Are we late?"

"No, but I want a good spot near the front." Carla snapped her arm the other direction and motioned over the gathering crowd by the park's big gazebo. The town's showcase feature, a wide and lazy river, rippled in the background.

Wiley swallowed and focused on the water. He tried not to look at the bus and the huge portrait of Kit emblazoned on the side, grinning and carefree, surrounded by sparkles and swags of tulle.

Kit, youngest of the Leydon brothers: voted most popular and most likely to succeed, now a superstar reality show wedding planner and Wiley's first crush and first awareness he was wired to crush like whoa on other boys. Over the years, Kit's eldest brother had come to the house to do some yardwork and chores for his grandma, and sometimes Kit would tag along and hang out. It gave Wiley an in with their grade's most popular kid, and Wiley had considered them friends growing up.

Kit had flown like a shot from Odalia immediately after graduation, and they'd lost touch. But that's what happened—people drifted. Even friends. Wiley had other things to worry about once in college and then moving to new places to start new jobs. He figured being a famous television personality had to be doubly busy and distracting, if not more.

Carla wanted to push into the cluster of people and get closer, but Wiley hung back. "You elbow through them if you want, but I can see fine from here."

"If we hang back, how am I going to catch Kit's eye as they make his big announcement?"

"I think it makes more sense to stand to the side and literally catch him as he walks offstage. Everyone will be up there trying to catch his eye. We can be positioned right here and nab him after it's over."

Carla blinked. "Hey, that's actually good. We'll do that." She planted her feet and rolled her hips. At Wiley's look she said, "Gotta stay limber and ready to lunge."

It did sound good. Reasonable. Way better than telling Carla *he* didn't want to accidentally catch Kit's eye and flail and look ridiculous or….

Or worse, have Kit's eye pass over him without a flicker of recognition.

He sighed but told himself it wouldn't be Kit's fault. Ten years was a long time.

"Excuse me—Coy?"

Wiley hadn't heard that nickname in years.

"You're Wiley Grey, correct?"

Wiley's heart dropped so fast it bounced off the ground and lodged in his throat. Light-headed anticipation surged through him, and a huge grin curled across his face as he turned.

And promptly choked on disappointment.

His grin faltered and he coughed. "Holt, isn't it?" It was Holt without a doubt, but it seemed better to match Holt's polite inquiry. He cast about for a reason why his grin had turned into a grimace and said, "You surprised me. No one's called me Coy in ages."

At least that much was true.

"So you remember me. I'm relieved I was right in remembering you." Holt's tone was clipped, and he inclined his head. "Maybe you hate the nickname. I'm sorry. It's the first thing that popped into my head when I saw you."

For no good reason, Wiley's grin returned.

Holt smiled too, and disarming crinkles appeared around his striking blue-white eyes, making him suddenly friendly and familiar. His thick waves of light blond hair looked silver when the sun hit them, and Wiley had to tilt back a bit to meet his gaze. Details Wiley hadn't noticed before, but then he hadn't really paid attention.

"Do you?"

"What?" Wiley's gaze had strayed to the breadth of Holt's shoulders, making a ridiculous display under an expensively casual blue button-up. "Oh no. I don't hate it. But it's been long enough I wasn't sure you were talking to me at first."

He had never liked it. Did hate it. At twelve and trying to hang with the cool kids, he'd worried it sounded dorky and juvenile, especially since it was inspired by a cartoon. But Kit had thought of it, an inelegant play on his name using an imprecise truncation of the hapless animated roadrunner victim, so he'd agreed it was super clever and accepted it with a smile.

He'd wondered if it should be said *ki* not *coy* all considered, but whatever. It had worked for Kit, so that meant it had worked for him.

Kit had called him Coy for maybe a week before losing interest. Holt heard it while at the house doing something for Grandma, studied him, and pronounced he did look like a dusky little coyote, with his brown eyes and red-brown hair. From then on Holt called him that, usually with a ruffling of said red-brown hair and a friendly wink. Wiley found he hadn't minded when Holt entered the house in grubby work clothes and said, "Heya, Coy," before drinking all the cold lemonade Grandma always had at the ready.

Come to think of it, Wiley didn't remember being called Coy since Holt left town, disappearing off to college not long after Wiley started to really notice how much he really liked Kit.

Wiley was counting the buttons downward toward Holt's narrow hips when Carla nudged him.

"Oh, right. Holt, this is Carla." He nodded at her and then at Holt. "She was in Kit's and my class in school. Carla—Holt is Kit's brother."

"You're better looking in person than on camera." She grinned, and from her, that was somehow charming instead of terrible. "And oh, I remember now. There's three of you with... Brent in the middle. Isn't there? And Kit's the baby?"

"That he is. And thank you." Holt made a wry face. "Making me the senior?"

Wiley wasn't sure what to attribute Holt's tone to, called out as older or some shade at Kit. He tilted his head and got a quick eyeful of Holt's commanding posture and, uh, surprisingly great ass. Holt caught his eye and he straightened.

"Eldest, but not old," Wiley offered.

Holt's gaze brightened at that.

Carla popped her lips and stuck out her hand. "No, you're years from falling apart. And I thought so. Hi. Carla of CarlaCakes—we're on the square downtown?"

"Good to meet you, Carla. I read about your bakery." Holt allowed Carla to lever his hand several times before carefully extracting it to fish his phone from a pocket.

"Wait, you did?" Carla shot Wiley a speaking look and waggled her eyebrows. "Soooo, does that mean you guys are in town for an episode? One you'll be needing a cake for?"

Holt paused his phone tapping, and Carla held out her palms.

"I'm not asking for any spoilers or secret intel. I'm just on the hustle, same as you. And saying we can whip up a dream of a cake and to keep us in mind." She elbowed Wiley. "Can't we?"

"We?" Holt lowered the phone and pinned Wiley with a look. "Did you become a baker too? I thought it was all art all the time—weren't you going to draw comic books or animation or something?"

Wiley's stomach butterflies surged to knock around his ribs. No one remembered the comic-book thing. Not even Grandma had talked about it once he moved back here to take care of her when she got sick. He used to fill notebook after notebook with drawings, copying his favorite panels from comics and making up his own characters in alien worlds, with outfits and weaponry and galactic pets. But that stopped the minute after graduation and reality set in.

"He helps out when I've got a big order and on Sunday mornings—brunch rush, you know." Carla made big eyes. "Wait, you don't. You should come by on Sunday and see for yourself!"

Holt kept focus on Wiley a moment more and then shifted to smile at Carla. "I'm going to be pulled in all directions while here, but Sunday brunch sounds nice. Maybe I can make something work. Thank you." He seemed on the verge of asking something else when an alarm on his phone sounded, music crackled from the speakers lining the gazebo front, and the crowd started to murmur.

The hair on the back of Wiley's neck stood on end, and he craned to see past Holt to the bus right as Kit emerged, sparkly and gorgeous and waving at everyone.

Holt cleared his throat. "Well, that's my cue. Good to see you, Coy—Wiley—and pleasure to make your reacquaintance, Carla."

"Samesies. And c'mon over Sunday. Don't forget," Carla said, voice rising above the noise.

Wiley nodded distractedly, his gaze riveted to Kit. Even the scattered clouds cooperated, parting in the exact right place so the sun bathed Kit in full light as he approached.

Kit's gaze traveled over the crowd and Wiley was pretty sure it paused on him. It could be from Holt standing there, but Wiley was sure he saw a spark of recognition. He went onto his toes and waved and, showing admirable restraint, didn't rush over for a tackle-hug.

Holt moved away from him and a draft cooled Wiley's skin. He broke from ogling Kit and followed Holt's deliberate progress to the gazebo with a brief frown.

"He's way better looking than I remembered. What a hunk of hunky man. I'm talking tree-climbing. Oof," Carla said in his ear. "Of course I was just a kid, but still."

"I always knew." Wiley nodded, his gaze back on Kit. He couldn't quite believe that Kit was here and maybe they could meet and talk and catch up on old times and Kit would remember what an amazing friend he'd been and they'd laugh over memories and Kit couldn't help but fall in love with him. Or feel some infatuation back.

The theme music from Kit's show swelled, and Kit did a short cha-cha to it and got everyone to clap along. Wiley swallowed as Kit danced right past him, cute and deeply dimpled in a pastel floral suit, blue skinny tie and pocket square, and matching nail polish. Kit held up both hands as he ran up the gazebo stairs and Holt gave him long-suffering but fond high-fives. A small camera crew joined the brothers onstage, and they moved as a unit, clearly used to following and being followed.

"I meant Holt, Wiley."

That broke through Wiley's reverie enough to have him give her a sidelong look. "You did? He was?"

Carla rolled her eyes. "You're hopeless. And blushing."

"It's sunny and hot and there's no breeze."

"It's June and there's a strong, refreshing wind coming off the river."

"Whatever."

Mayor Anderson spoke first, gushing welcomes and about the excitement the whole town felt to be graced by the famous Leydon brothers' visit and what all they'd thrown together in preparation. Wiley ignored her in favor of watching Kit waiting in the wings, and liked how he could linger on Kit's features and reminisce without anyone knowing or thinking it was weird.

Kit was all motion and magnetism, even standing doing nothing while Anderson droned on. Wiley settled in to catalog every little thing but he got distracted by Holt, tall and broad and steady, calmly talking into Kit's ear.

Saying something that caught Kit's attention and that Holt didn't seem to quite like.

Both their gazes darted toward the audience, and pinpricks danced over Wiley's skin, because he was certain they were talking about him.

Holt was tight-lipped and Kit had a look Wiley remembered well—it was the same as when Kit had discovered a way to wriggle out of trouble. Usually only enough wriggling to save himself and usually trouble of his own making.

"So, without further ado, I'm honored to introduce the stars of *Marry Me!*—let's give Kit and Holt a big ovation and hear what they have to say." The mayor raised both arms and then swooped them down in a flourish as she stepped aside.

Applause and cheers rose, and during the crescendo, Kit crossed in front of Holt and took the mic with an enormous grin.

"Thank you, Mayor. And wow! Hello Odalia, it's amazing to be home again." Kit put a hand over his heart. "And it is home, no matter how long I've been away, especially with all of you here to greet us. Fire Chief Peters and Doc Fielding—I thought you were going to retire, ha-ha—and the old Hash It Out diner crew."

Kit pointed toward the individuals named as he spoke and already had everyone eating out of his hand.

"Seeing you all here makes this announcement so much easier to do, and I can't think of a better way to share it with the world." Kit's smile turned tremulous, and he let out a long breath. "We've teased a big announcement for weeks, and although the speculation has been pretty entertaining, it is important and personal. Something I'm glad we can share." He half covered his mouth with his hand and leaned forward conspiratorially. "Someone even had the idea I was going to quit—spoiler alert, I'm not!"

Ripples of laughter chased his comments, but tension had tightened around the group.

"As you all know, I'm in the marrying business. I mean, I've married so many people in the last five years I'm glad monogrammed towels are out of fashion." Kit raised a placating hand at the errant groans from the crowd. "But. We've come here because this time is different. Yes, we love Odalia, and yes, we're filming a very special episode so we can celebrate with our hometown family, but one specific person brought the show here again. I'm about to marry someone wonderful. Someone incredible. Someone you all know maybe better than you do me."

Kit tilted his outstretched palm and curled his fingers in a beckoning gesture, and the audience, as if on cue, parted in a widening vee until it stopped at Wiley.

Thundering blood filled Wiley's head like white noise and he stood rooted, his field of vision telescoped on Kit on the stage, beaming at him like he was the most magical person in the world.

Wiley flashed hot and then cold. He had no idea what Kit was talking about. He didn't need a wedding planner. In Odalia. He had no one to marry and probably never would.

Friends and neighbors and a few people he didn't recognize were turned to him, some of the ladies dewy-eyed and swooning, and Kit still waited on the stage.

Carla ground her elbow into Wiley's side, but he could only shake his head and listen as his wits rattled around.

"Wiley?" Holt materialized out of nowhere. "There's no explaining, so just trust me if you can, and go with this," he murmured and wrapped a powerful arm around Wiley's shoulders.

Wiley was too stunned to argue and then he was in the gazebo, awkwardly patting Kit's back after Kit squealed and hugged him too tightly.

"I know I'm usually the one quietly solving all the problems and meeting every grand gesture promise Kit creates in the background of any given episode, but what Kit said is true. He's agreed to take on marrying me to my hometown sweetheart, Wiley Grey." Holt turned from the microphone to smile, quiet and besotted-seeming, at Wiley. "Isn't that right?"

Kit stiffened next to him and made a short noise of annoyance. Wiley turned to Kit for guidance, but Kit ignored his mute plea, instead flashing a dark look at Holt. If Wiley hadn't been watching Kit he'd have missed it, because after a beat Kit relaxed and grinned again. Kit pushed Wiley—not quite gently—toward Holt.

"Hi," Holt said after gathering Wiley close again, almost intimate but more for the audience's benefit. He was steady and open, seeming to will Wiley into not freaking totally out and diving off the back of the stage into the river.

Holt tightened his arm when Wiley unconsciously glanced behind them at the appealing thought. His smile was more chagrin than humor, and he closed his eyes and touched Wiley's hairline with the briefest, softest of kisses.

Wiley unexpectedly shivered from that spot all the way to his toes.

Holt pulled back, stood still a breath, and then lifted his microphone.

"Oh. My. Gosh. Are they not the most adorable thing? I can't stand it!" Kit called, and the interruption pivoted all attention back to him.

Wiley had the feeling Kit was telling the truth with the last part.

"That's right, Odalia, we're here so I can plan the wedding of Holt and Wiley's dreams! What do you say, folks? Marry me?"

Everyone cheered and chanted "Marry me" several times until Kit motioned for them to quiet again.

"And Holt—I think I know your answer, but you know the drill."

"Absolutely," Holt said without hesitation. "Marry me."

The crowd cheered louder at that.

"That leaves you, Wiley. Our mystery man of the hour—okay, past several months—now revealed." Kit's stare bored into Wiley.

He feverishly tried to compose witty or conciliatory refusals but only managed to draw a really huge blank. Wiley considered the river again and wondered how far the current would take him. If he played it right, maybe he could wash up in a whole different state and then change his name and never look back.

Holt rubbed a hand up and down Wiley's back and then cupped it over his shoulder.

He looked up into Holt's eyes and without meaning to said, "Uh, marry me."

The microphone barely picked him up but that didn't matter. Everyone hooted and music began to play, and Wiley looked into the crowd to see Carla, staring at him as wide-eyed as he felt. She planted her hands on her hips and mouthed the letters "WTF?" at him.

He wished he had any clue.

The rest of the announcement was a blur. Holt kept hold of him the whole time as they shifted backward so Kit could take center stage again. Wiley nodded and smiled and struggled not to think about the implications of what he'd agreed to while also obsessing over what he'd just agreed to.

"Thank you so much, Odalia! We start filming tomorrow—that's right, this whole episode is going to be a live event, step by step, here with you. So see you bright and early. Thanks for saying y-e-s!"

As Kit spelled yes aloud, the audience joined in.

Then Anderson was shaking his hand and offering congratulations, as did the others on stage. Wiley only half registered it and Holt's grip moving to his elbow to lead him down the stairs and onto the grass.

He just kept smiling and nodding and waving until they were safely shut into the bus, sans camera crew.

It was very quiet all of a sudden and Wiley didn't know what to do with himself.

No one seemed to.

A loud banging made them each jump.

Kit laughed weirdly and Holt squeezed his arm, then peered outside and opened the door.

Carla barged in and Holt got the door shut behind her before anyone else could get a peek inside. She flapped her hands in baffled protest until finally she found some words.

"Oh my God, Wiley. What have you done?"

He looked from Carla to Holt to Kit and back.

"I said yes."

HOLT couldn't quite believe what he'd done. He couldn't believe Wiley had said yes.

The crowd outside still buzzed with the news. What a homecoming. At least he'd managed to get the camera crew and Janet, their sometimes-too-on-the-spot PA, ensconced in the front of the bus and got the privacy barrier closed between them.

Aside from Carla's incessant tapping, inside the bus was silent and tense. She sat perched on the galley kitchen counter and kept sending speaking glances at Wiley, who still stood where Holt had finally let go to take a seat on the low bench at the back of the bus. Wiley pointedly did not answer her. Then she'd turn and glare at Holt, but he knew better than to start ahead of Kit's building steam. He was waiting, counting to one hundred, because Kit's silence wouldn't last long, and it was more efficient to let him erupt before trying to make logical sense of anything.

His terse, rushed conversation with Kit before the big announcement played on a loop in his mind. Him mentioning to Kit that Wiley—your old friend Wiley—was in attendance. Kit asking him to point Wiley out, and once he had, Kit studying Wiley speculatively before nodding with satisfaction. "This could fix things. I know how to make this work," Kit said, with that certain gleam in his eyes that always spelled mischief, at best.

Holt had done very quick math and then, with an impulse he couldn't fully explain, had stepped over Kit's idea and taken it for himself.

He looked over at Wiley, who happened to be staring at him. Holt motioned to the bench next to him. Wiley ignored the offer. He smiled and it felt flat and wry. When Kit shot out a low breath, Holt lifted a hand and counted on his fingers down from five and then made a fist.

"Okay? What the what was that?" Kit's voice rose as he spoke. He stomped past Wiley, flailed a huge wave to indicate the world beyond the bus, and then stomped back to where Holt sat.

"The start of our next episode?" Holt offered blandly.

Kit's eye roll encompassed his whole body. "Cute, Holty. Now answer me for real." He paused a breath but then plowed on. "How is that the episode? How will this work? You can't possibly be marrying...." He glanced at Wiley. "Uh, our friend."

"Wiley," Holt reminded him, and didn't miss how Wiley stiffened to an awkward full-attention stance. He also didn't miss how Wiley's hands twitched, and then Wiley started to move.

Holt was up and across the bus in two long strides. He stood not quite blocking Wiley's path—but an impediment Wiley would have to decide to get around to flee the bus—and waited. Wiley stopped fidgeting but didn't relax. Holt could hardly blame him.

"I'm really sorry." Holt had nothing better to say, but it seemed a good place to start. "Come sit, have some water and we have snacks, and let me explain."

He gazed down at Wiley and noticed the freckles and moles from Wiley's cheek to jaw to neck and remembered them, like he'd always known they were there, how he'd thought they looked like the Big Dipper with the North Star right by Wiley's nose.

A memory of being in Wiley's house stirred in him. Wiley, friendly and with an easier laugh without Kit around, young and shy and alone in the world save for his grandma. Holt had felt a little sorry for both of them, although the peppery grandma would have resented that.

Wiley continued to stand there, stiff and awkward and probably full of regret.

"Please," Holt added. He stepped back but let a hand fall on Wiley's shoulder and, without thinking about it, dug his thumb in as a reassuring massage.

Wiley was lean but not scrawny. Holt's hand spanned Wiley's shoulder, warm in the cup of his palm. Wiley's muscles flexed under his touch, and the sensation tickled up through his arm. He pulled away as if singed.

Holt flexed his hand and turned to search the kitchenette cupboards for the snacks he mentioned. He piled various bars and trail mix packs and small chocolates on the table bolted to the wall and separating the bench and kitchen spaces, and then got one of every drink from the minifridge.

He opened a can of orange-flavored sparkling water and offered Wiley the cherry-flavored one. Wiley, if he remembered correctly, couldn't resist cherry anything.

"Carla?" he asked as Wiley continued to resist.

She kept glaring at him but took a granola bar, a handful of chocolates, and a cola. She dropped onto the bench seat beside the table and started drumming her fingers.

Holt didn't exactly want her involved in this, but it was obviously too late to prevent that. She had to know the moment he'd fake-proposed that everything was a sham, so the best course was to include her. Otherwise she could go telling the world, thinking she was protecting Wiley, and that would be even worse than the current bind they were in.

"So you're marrying Wiley? You stealing the spotlight is how you think this should go?" Kit nabbed a protein bar and kept pacing.

"I focused the spotlight back onto you, Kit," Holt answered in his very reasonable tone while continuing to watch Wiley, who was a half step closer and eyeing the cherry water. He casually resituated so there was room on the bench next to him for Wiley to sit.

Kit stopped at that. "Explain," he said and took a pointed bite of his no-carb seaweed bar.

"You'll have to handle this episode on your own. The only host, the most camera time. I'll be too busy making wedding decisions to do anything else. So, no last-minute carpentry fix or event space rework or finding a ring-bearing elephant because you promised the bride that would happen."

"That elephant lives a wonderful life in a reserve, and that episode raised so much money for them!" Kit made his particular little noise of impatience. He turned to Carla. "Honestly, it was the best. Did you see that one?"

Carla, to her credit, managed to nod without hesitation. "The bride was overjoyed."

"Yes, she was. Which is always exactly the goal." Kit turned back to Holt. "Maybe you facilitated getting the elephant, I mean, you are the nuts-and-bolts guy. But it was my idea and my magic that brought Gertie's performance seamlessly into those nuptials."

"Sure. I'm happy to let you have that. But it's also way off topic." Holt opened a bag of trail mix with deliberate slowness to let Kit get past elephants and back to the argument he was carefully framing. "On topic is we should cancel the wedding. For starters and enders, this isn't exactly fair to Wiley, who more or less agreed under duress."

Kit flapped his hands impatiently. "Blink twice if Holt has taken you hostage, dearie," he said to Wiley.

Wiley cracked the first real smile Holt had seen since the crowd parted during the presser.

A twinge of annoyance at their humor pinched Holt, but he said reasonably, "I step aside, you take apologetic lead and be the one to rescue everything, and production figures out another way to feature Odalia. We blame cold feet or leak that we ran off to elope because the pressure was too much and then, just never elope."

Holt could bear the brunt of the humiliation and bad press. Even shoulder what might become a ratings disaster. He actively didn't care what was said about him, but Kit would, and he wouldn't ever agree to walk away once setting this into motion in front of Odalia and everybody. So he'd take the hit. But he needed for Kit to think Kit was making the final decision about the episode, and he could tell the wheels were turning in Kit's scheming brain. He hoped they were going in the right direction.

Kit came to a halt and crossed his arms. He tapped his index finger in the divot above his lips in a characteristic tell that he was giving something great thought, and Holt's expectancy rose.

"Tempting, but no. Big absolute no."

Holt continued to play it cool. "I'll make the announcement and everything. You don't have to do any of the messy stuff," he offered.

"That is not what I mean. We are definitely not canceling the wedding."

Holt suppressed a sigh. Kit's scheming wheels were indeed cranking, but full speed ahead was not the intention here.

"Again, I refer you to Wiley." Holt looked at Wiley, who sat peering into the open can of sparkling cherry water. "Coy?" he asked quietly.

Wiley looked up with a surprising expression of determination.

A shiver of premonition that he wasn't getting out of this at all crawled up Holt's back.

"Yes, Wiley. Oh, Wiley! What do you have to say? Can you help us out?" Kit flopped onto the couch at the back of the bus. "Not to be dramatic," he said dramatically, "but the truth is—and it's only right you know it—I thought this wedding episode would be for me and my honeydew, who I'd believed was about to propose but turned out to be a rat. I never would have involved this backwater or little old you otherwise!"

Holt didn't wince at Kit's breezy insult. He'd wince nonstop if he let things like that bother him anymore. Kit was overall kind and well-meaning and thoughtless. But Wiley's frown made him instinctively pivot the heel of his hand against the tabletop toward Wiley's tensely curled fist.

He meant to pat once or tap their knuckles together but wound up covering Wiley's hand with his. The contact jarred him with a short, sharp bolt of heat. Wiley coughed and straightened, not looking back to see Holt's stilted smile or Holt withdrawing and rubbing his hand against his perfectly creased brown work pants.

Must be the dry, recirculated air inside the bus. And nerves.

Wiley's nerves, because there was no reason for Holt to be nervous.

Kit carried on, oblivious to the slight or anything else. "But you could rescue me. The show." He splayed his hand over his heart. "I'm seeing it so clearly now and it's just too good. I thought that I could be some bashful bride returned to his hometown for orange blossoms and roses, but no, this is way better. Me fabulously sharing with everyone this romance I nurtured in hush-hush secret because you're both publicity shy—so presh—but masterminding this to ensure my best friends still have the wedding of their dreams? Far superior and so much my strengths. You had good instincts for once, Holty." He sat upright. "We can do this. Can't we? Tell me we can."

"Can get married? I think that's a big ask, considering." Holt shook his head. Kit for sure thought he'd come up with this whole thing, but in all the wrong ways. "We should have canceled or delayed the announcement to get things sorted out after your 'amazing getaway so Blaine could pop the question' turned out to be a 'guilt break-up pity trip.' And you definitely should not have dragged Wiley into this."

"I drag? I?" Kit let his seaweed bar wrapper fall on the table. "I'm not who asked him to marry me in front of everyone, without any prior warning or plan."

Instead of arguing, Holt scooted the wrapper to him and opened it fully along its sealed edges, tied it into a tight knot, and set it alongside his to throw away later.

"You called him onstage. That's all I'll say." Holt gave Kit a warning look that somehow still worked after all these years. Older-brother powers ran deep. "But filming the show—live, I am now learning, thanks for that—with the idea we're getting married is going too far. Way too far."

A long silence followed where no one agreed with him.

He'd stepped in so Wiley wasn't completely railroaded by Kit, known the moment Kit had asked him to point Wiley out in the crowd what was brewing and that it'd go horribly awry if he allowed it, but that's where it was supposed to end.

The crawling sensation of what was now dread made it to his nape, and he ran his hands through his hair.

"You could always film the episode and claim cold feet at the end. Run away to do the elope-nonelope thing," Carla piped up. "I mean, it seems to me that Kit has a show to salvage, this town could use the boost, and I have a cake to bake. Given Wiley agrees and doesn't mind a few weeks—months—of speculation and gossip and sympathy once back in Odalia husbandless. Of course."

"Of course," Holt said dryly. "Your bakery gets featured, Kit gets to be fairy godmother, but what does that get Wiley?" He squeezed his thigh to stop from reaching out to Wiley again but he met, and held, Wiley's gaze. "You do *not* have to agree."

Wiley didn't hesitate. "I will if you will."

Kit gasped exultantly and Carla bounced on her seat. Holt's heart sank.

"I don't want the show to be ruined, and Carla is an incredible baker and…. We can go on that nonelope thing. That's a good idea. I don't know why it can't work any less than all the other scripted 'reality' stuff you guys do. I am desperate to get out of Odalia." Wiley's jaw set as he studied Holt for several minutes, then asked seriously, "What can *you* gain? I mean, if we're all agreeing to terms here."

The answer came to Holt so easily, but he was still surprised by it.

He'd never wanted to be in front of the camera. Coming on to work behind the scenes had been a fluke on its own, but one episode in the second season, everything was going so wrong he'd wound up heavily featured as he'd problem-solved and built custom enchanted forest backdrops and was the only one who could talk Kit down from the ledge.

That episode proved to be an instant hit. Holt and Kit were perfect foils for each other, him deliberate and steady and Kit an excitable jumble of energy, but not so extreme it made the other look bad. There was also apparently something about him in a low-slung tool belt and the leather suspenders he preferred that struck quite the chord with viewers. Holt had been in front of the camera ever since.

He'd wanted off almost as long but hadn't found any good outs.

"Holt," Kit whined. "We can do this! You can do this. For the greater good."

"Yours, perhaps," Holt said flatly.

Kit lifted one shoulder unapologetically.

"Maybe you don't want to do this with me." Wiley emphasized the last word, and his hands had curled into fists again. "Not like I don't understand that."

It made Holt almost angry Wiley would skew it that way.

"You have to want something," Carla cut in. "We all do, and that doesn't make you a bad person. Neither does filming a show where we all know the score. Even if the audience doesn't." She thought it over a moment. "At least I don't think it does."

"It so absolutely does not," Kit said emphatically. "We'll make a great team and make a great show. I believe in us. Holt. Please."

Score one back for little-brother powers, because although Holt mostly ignored Kit's wheedling tone, it still managed to jab sharply just under his heart.

Holt licked his lips and glanced at Wiley, who watched him lick his lips. He cleared his throat and squared his shoulders and fought off an errant blush. He wasn't used to making terms or demands—he usually negotiated or met them.

He braced for impact and said, "We make it my final episode."

"Fine."

"Fine?" Kit's mild response stunned Holt. "That's it?"

"God." Kit rolled his eyes. "Like I want you moping around on set like a miserable prisoner and having to cajole you on camera after sharing this?"

"But if I leave the show, the show might end." It would for certain end, and they both knew it, but Holt wasn't going to say that aloud.

"So it ends," Kit dismissed. "There's other things, other opportunities. Fabulous doesn't simply disappear—unless it's choreographed and in a cloud of glitter, natch."

Holt didn't know what to make of Kit's reaction, but he accepted it. For now.

"Okay, right. Holt gets to announce that this wedding-nonwedding made him realize it's time to retire and off he goes, gracefully into that gray sunset. Carla is our featured baker—which was a given anyway, I mean, look at our preproduction notes. Swearsies. Wiley gets a trip to anywhere for at least a month aaaand we'll toss in a makeover." Kit winked and shimmied his shoulders like that was so great and Wiley should be thrilled.

From the corner of his eye, Holt saw Wiley droop again.

"Wardrobe for the honeymoon maybe, because otherwise he doesn't need much."

Kit's eyebrow arched sharply.

"What? It's true," Holt said, matter-of-fact. It was. Wiley was going to make an appealing groom for the camera. Thick, dark hair, not as red as he remembered but undertones remained, with a loose curl that swept up from Wiley's forehead and curled under his ears, a dusky complexion and that scatter of cute moles, a lush mouth he didn't seem to be aware of, and shy but intelligent velvet-brown eyes.

Not that he was making and keeping an inventory. No, it was merely the kind of thing Holt noticed after so many years in the biz.

"What do you get?" Holt asked, effectively changing the subject.

"A likely ratings bonanza, a favor for my big bro who came on board the show and helped it thrive season after season even though he apparently hates it, a launch into something else." Kit's eyes sparkled with mercenary charm. He definitely already had some ideas about what the something else would be.

"Wait, have you wanted me gone?"

"No!" Kit huffed and reached across the tight space to ruffle Holt's hair. "It's just that we're agreed, silly. So." He tugged Holt's hair and then thrust his hand between the group. "All in?"

Carla put her hand on top of Kit's, and after a moment Wiley stacked his on top.

Holt considered it. He didn't love the idea of bargaining based on deception, but the part of him urgent to agree, banging in the back of his mind like a wind-up monkey with cymbals, was near impossible to ignore.

Everyone here knew the score. He wouldn't be tricking anyone who could get hurt.

He put his hand over Wiley's, careful to barely make contact. "All in."

"THAT'S it? A trip?" Carla huffed and slapped a box of day-old pastries onto the counter between them.

"Gosh, sorry. I was kind of put on the spot without any chance to prepare a list of demands there. What should I have asked for, a million dollars?"

"Yes! Maybe? I don't know." She sighed and sagged onto the tall wooden stool she'd dragged from the kitchen to sit facing Wiley on the customer side of the bakery bar. "What a mess."

"Imagine how much messier it could get." Wiley considered it and then shook his head. "On second thought...."

"Yeah. It's a good thing I closed early so we could go hear the big announcement." She bit into a chocolate croissant and then stared into the center thoughtfully. "Or not, considering."

Wiley picked at a bear claw and didn't know how to answer. Part of him was elated at what he'd done. It was a tiny part. The rest was having a very quiet, but very total, freak-out.

Carla had tried to hustle him here the moment they'd escaped the bus—and escape was the right word, because press and fans had staked the thing out, desperate to get another glimpse of him.

In the end Holt had maneuvered them into a nearby SUV complete with a driver and dark-tinted windows. He'd had Wiley tucked under an arm and pushed Carla ahead of them, and they squished together on the middle bench, Wiley almost in Holt's lap.

He trembled at the memory.

Wiley didn't enjoy being under that much scrutiny, but that wouldn't change anytime soon.

"Hey." Carla nudged Wiley's neglected mug of coffee an inch closer to him. "Are you going to be okay?"

"Did I make a huge mistake?"

Carla shrugged. "Too late now."

That brought Wiley up short. He straightened and quit imagining worst-case scenarios, one after the other. She was right.

"Look on the bright side—you're going to get a whole lot of quality time with Kit."

Wiley nodded and sipped his coffee. But when he thought about the whirlwind of the last few hours, all he could picture was Holt.

"So true. I can always count on you with that silver lining," he said, not even sounding convincing to himself.

Carla eyed him and then leaned way over to grab the coffeepot and the notepad and pen she always kept by the bakery case. She topped off their mugs and tapped the paper with a finger. "Okay, then. Let's make a plan."

"Some marketing thing for the bakery?"

Her lips flattened together. "No, a make-it-through-this-still-mostly-sane-so-you-can-go-on-your-trip plan."

"That's probably a good idea." Wiley had no clue where to start.

"It's a great idea. Genius, even." Carla made a list of numbers with bold dashes after them, brought her pen back up to one, and looked at him expectantly. "Your turn."

A snicker bubbled up in Wiley and spilled over until he was laughing too hard to answer.

"Oh, come on. It wasn't that funny. It wasn't funny at all."

"I had to do something. My nerves are shot." Wiley's laughter faded, and the release left him wrung out. He took the pen from her and began doodling around the edges of the paper. Drawing always helped him focus and relax.

"Maybe we don't need a numbered and ordered plan. But we should lay some groundwork. Code words, secret gestures, you know, like in crime movies, so if something is really heavy or tough for you, you adjust your tie and I come running in."

"When do I ever wear ties?"

"That's not what I mean, and you know it." Carla poked at her phone to check the time. "We've been in here three hours. I don't think anyone followed us here, so you can probably go home." She boxed the remaining pastries and slid them to Wiley. "We don't have to plan anything. Go get some rest and we can figure it out starting tomorrow. I mean, we're not half bad at winging things. Look at this place!"

Carla's cheer was forced but Wiley appreciated it, even if he was starting to go numb from overload.

"You did okay with the bakery, I'll give you that."

"We did," Carla corrected. "I got the crazy notion to open it, but you've helped me every step to getting in the black. I can help you with this."

Wiley didn't tell her getting the bakery off the ground with nothing but a rent break from the downtown development grant and Carla's knack for addictive cupcakes had been a lifesaver to him, providing distraction and a challenge after his grandmother's death, something to do that wasn't sorting through decades of accumulated stuff.

"I'd say you owe me, given what you said on the bus to keep Kit's own crazy notion rolling." He smiled as he asked, but things didn't seem as clear as they had when he'd agreed to this. Wiley lifted the box of treats in thanks and headed for the door. He peered out past the shade Carla had pulled down after their arrival but didn't see anything, so he unlocked the door and put a cautious foot outside.

"After today there'll probably be a run on danishes and donuts, and gossip. Come help me—get here an hour early," Carla called.

He waved acknowledgment and shook his head but didn't mind. He liked being useful and reliable, and liked that others relied on him.

Given today's outcome, he might like that too much.

But much as he might want to, he couldn't blame Carla or her ridiculous year-of-saying-yes babble. He rarely said no when someone asked for a favor or needed what he thought he could provide. It was how he ended up back in Odalia, after all.

Wiley kept an eye open as he hurried down Main Street and turned the corner onto Wren Avenue. He darted through a gap in a tall hedge and into the backyards he always cut through on his walk to and from the bakery. The fifth backyard led to Sparrow Avenue, and two blocks up Sparrow sat Grandma's house.

It wasn't fancy. The biggest houses in Odalia sat on huge lots along the winding road leading to and from the heart of downtown. Every block behind that road, the houses and lots got smaller and smaller. When Grandma and her husband married—a grandfather Wiley had never met—their tidy starter home had been on the edge of town.

But he liked the sturdy cracker box, cedar-sided house. It was familiar. He'd grown up here. Now it belonged to him, for all he was trying to decide what to do with it.

Wiley hunched behind a huge oak tree and eyed the house. No news trucks were parked outside or reporters camped on the lawn, but he broke into a run and didn't relax until he had the front door shut behind him.

"Whaaaa!" he yelled when something huge and dark loomed toward him from the kitchen.

The overhead light came on and flooded the dim hall. Holt lifted his hands in apology.

Wiley clapped a hand over his heart and let out a rough breath. His gaze darted around the room as if Kit and the camera crew would be lurking to catch his reaction, but managed to gather his wits enough to say, "Did you handyman a break-in?"

Holt smiled ruefully and turned his wrist to reveal a key held in his hand. It looked ridiculously tiny flashing against his palm. "You keep the spare in the same place GB did." He took a slow step and put it on the narrow table *set* against the back wall of the living room and stood in the connecting doorway between the kitchen and the rest of the house. "Sorry, I just got here or I'd have turned on a light or something. I didn't intend to scare you, or even beat you here. But since I did and I found the spare and I didn't want to be creeping around or wind up in a photospread creeping around, here I am. Already inside."

Wiley hadn't heard *GB* in years. It's what his friends growing up and the kids in the neighborhood called his grandma—Bess, who was too old-fashioned to let them call her that, but had no use for standing on formality either.

"Understood." Wiley nodded and found he didn't mind Holt had simply come right in. He liked it, even. "Want some lemonade?"

Holt smiled. "That'd be great." He rolled into the kitchen and sat at one of Wiley's favorite spots in the house, a bench built into the corner of windows overlooking the backyard still thick with Grandma's flowers and interlacing ivy.

With two glasses in hand, Wiley turned to set them on the island and tilted his head at Holt. "You built that, didn't you." He shook his head and rooted in the fridge for the lemonade. "This has been a day of remembering things I haven't thought of in decades."

"Decades? Whew, you do think of me as old, after all." Holt's tone was flat, but his eyes twinkled. He accepted a glass of lemonade and raised it.

By habit Wiley tapped his glass to Holt's and pulled out a chair to sit opposite. "Okay, so it hasn't been *decades* since you built the bench or were the only person to call me Coy, but that's also not the only memories stirred up by everything that's happened. Which—wow, has been a lot. Are we sure it's only been one day?"

"Coy suits you. Still does." Holt's gaze went from Wiley's hair, to his eyes, to his lips, held a moment, and then it shifted to the garden. "You've kept the house up nice. I noticed you painted the front door and shutters the dark gray you were always trying to convince GB would look good with the cedar."

"And?"

"And, it does. But that isn't a surprise given your artistic eye. The white and blue repaint looks good in here too."

Wiley was unaccountably pleased with Holt's approval, but then, Holt knew the history of the house and how stuck in her ways Grandma could be. It mattered more for someone like Holt to appreciate the differences.

"I don't think I ever saw it this... tidy, either."

Wiley's pleasure crashed.

He didn't need the Leydon brothers' sudden reappearance to dredge up memories.

Grandma could charitably have been called a collector, a vanguard of the upcycle movement, always finding new uses for boxes and bins and random findings. Not quite a hoarder—Grandma had strict cleanliness rules—but it was a house kept clean under constantly moving and growing piles of stuff. Endless stuff. Wiley hadn't had friends over often, and when they came over, they didn't stay long. He could easily recall Kit's mild but palpable distaste, and Kit's exaggerated willingness to be here *anyway*.

Cleaning it out had taken Wiley a year.

A year of decisions and frustration and doing his best to recycle or donate whatever he could, until he had whittled it down to what he liked and needed to live, and the rest he finally let himself drive to the dump and forget.

"I'm sorry again, Wiley. I didn't mean anything in that—you did your best as a kid, and I didn't ever care." Holt's hand, big and warm, covered Wiley's wrist. "Hurting your feelings is worse than scaring the devil out of you. Those big brown eyes of yours are dangerous." His eyes became steely, intense, and then Holt blinked and shifted back on the bench, taking his hand away.

Wiley shivered and flexed his wrist. For something to do, he got the pitcher of lemonade and a pack of cookies. He dumped them on a plate, neatly tied the emptied bag in a knot, and threw it in the trash.

"You do that too?" Holt indicated the knotted bag.

Wiley held a cookie in his mouth as he refilled their drinks and set the plate down. "No," he said around the cookie. "Starting with that, though, yes. It's smart."

Holt grinned and ate two cookies in one bite.

They munched in silence for a while as Wiley watched a bird flip leaves in a bug forage in the backyard.

Wiley didn't want to interrupt the easy mood—it was nice to have company, even if the company and reason was so strange—but when the cookies ran out, he pulled in a deep breath.

"So, you're here because…."

Holt turned to look at Wiley but kept his legs outstretched under the table parallel to the bench, and the twist in his shoulders emphasized their width.

Wiley swallowed and had a sip of tepid lemonade. "Remember, we start filming tomorrow? Ergo, we should decide on the basics about 'us' and how to handle any unknowns that crop up before that starts."

"Oh." Until that very moment, Wiley's mind had been full of angry question-bees. He stared at Holt and drew a blank.

When Holt huffed a low laugh, his eyelids lowered. Wiley wanted to reach out and check to make sure the length of Holt's eyelashes—too pale to be fully seen in the bright sun earlier today—were as long and silky as they seemed.

Instead he jammed his hands under his thighs. He let his gaze fall to the bench so he didn't keep staring and was hit with inspiration. "You sent me condolences when Grandma died. Since you knew her and all that makes sense, and I was actually here to get your kind note and thoughtful houseplant. Because houseplants keep you company afterwards and don't die slowly in a vase."

Holt frowned.

"Not good? Too much of a downer to build a fake romance around?" Wiley flushed with embarrassment at saying *romance* aloud. The fake part beforehand somehow didn't make it hit with less awkwardness.

"No, it is good. I was thinking that I wish I'd sent condolences and a friendly houseplant."

Holt feeling bad about that made Wiley feel completely better about everything.

"Don't say you're sorry again, please." Wiley held up his hands and laughed. "It's fine—more than fine—I didn't even run an obit. Grandma didn't want any of that."

Holt seemed on the verge of arguing, so Wiley jabbed a finger in the air.

"Okay, fine." Holt ran a thumb along the back of the bench. "So we were friends as kids, lost touch after going our separate ways to college—you went, right? What did you major in?"

"Art." Wiley rolled his eyes. "Animation and illustrating, although I got a communications minor as a failsafe. Hilariously I haven't used either." There was no humor in Wiley's voice.

"I'm glad you followed that dream all the way through a degree, though. That's cool. I wanted to make cabinets and reclaimed barn-door tables, so of course I got a degree in business." Holt chuckled, and the warm sound rolled around in Wiley's belly. "Somehow that made me think I needed a master's—which I didn't by the way, so I bailed after one semester—and then I bummed around honing my skills with apprenticeships and trade work. It was a good few years, camping and traveling, making driftwood shelves and custom kitchens, and saving to open my own shop. Never got to that, though."

"Kit and the show?"

Holt nodded. "Kit and the show. They had a shoestring budget, and Kit was desperate to impress the network and knew I'd be useful, and cheap. Not quite

what I'd envisioned from life, but I could use my hands
and make good stuff and people happy, so I'm not sorry
I let Kit rope me into it."

Wiley hummed agreement and considered how
Holt's hand engulfed the glass of lemonade and forced
himself to think about cabinetry. Which led him to
imagining Holt patiently sanding and smoothing a
length of wood. He coughed and stretched his neck.

He'd never been so distracted by anyone. They hadn't
even started filming and the stress was cracking him up.

"What do you do here?"

"Hm?" Wiley peeled his eyes from Holt's hands. He
blinked, thought about what Holt had asked, and said, "I
freelance design seasonal décor—figurines, ornaments
and wall art, craft kits for kids, stuff like that—for an
import company. And help at the bakery, obviously."

Holt narrowed his eyes. "That could work too."

"What could?"

"Let's say after reconnecting I mentioned needing
a design for something on the show, and you mentioned
you could do it, and over that process we started talking
and kept talking…."

"And one thing led to another," Wiley finished,
catching on. "That does work pretty well."

"Yeah, and it's enough. The simpler we keep this
the better."

Wiley made a sarcastic noise. "That you *can* say
again."

"Valid." Holt pursed his lips. "Who asked whom?"

"You asked me," Wiley said without hesitation.
"Your proposal was very practical, and I was delighted
to accept."

"Have you traveled much in the past few years?"

Wiley's shoulders hunched unconsciously, and he shook his head.

"I was trying to think about where I proposed. Right here is good." Holt dusted his fingers up under Wiley's on the table and caught Wiley's hand in his. "Wiley Grey, thank you for your delighted acceptance, you make me a very relieved and very happy man."

When Holt smiled, crinkles appeared around his eyes. Wiley sighed.

"Well, thank you for asking. It's good we wanted to keep it secret, so there's no rings to rush out and get, and since we both do messy work it's been easier not to wear them yet. I guess all that's left is to do this get not-married thing."

"The easy part."

"The totally easy part," Wiley agreed. He ignored the sinking sensation in his gut.

"Have you watched much of the show?"

Wiley shook his head.

"I suggest you binge the most recent two seasons. We follow the same format each and every wedding, so that will prep you for knowing what to expect. It'll also help us navigate around potential obstacles—we won't have to make up reasons to be on camera together or fabricate much more backstory. We can just interact naturally over cake."

"That's my favorite thing, interacting naturally over cake," Wiley deadpanned. Holt's flat expression made him laugh. "You're so matter-of-fact, and this is entirely, completely, patently ridiculous." He sobered. "And kind of scaring the hell out of me."

"It's probably good to be afraid of this. At least a little bit." Holt stretched, stood, and carried the empty plate and glasses to the counter. "And it's dark out, which means I can and should leave."

The sun had gone down and dusk was mellow in the comfortable old kitchen and enveloping the yard. Wiley hadn't even noticed. He had the urge to invite Holt to stay longer and watch some old episodes with him. He stifled that and followed Holt to the side door off the kitchen that led to the garden and a path alongside the house.

Holt opened the door and reached for the latch on the screen door but paused. He turned and suddenly they were very close, close enough so Wiley's nose bumped Holt's chest.

"What time should I be on set? And where is the set?" Wiley looked up. Beard stubble textured Holt's neck and jaw, and Wiley liked the effect. He promptly stopped thinking about it.

Holt went still for a beat and then shook his head. "I'll pick you up."

"At the bakery—Carla expects an early run on danishes and rubbernecking."

"I can't imagine she's wrong." Holt took a half step, hesitated, and then he let go of the screen door. He covered Wiley's shoulders with his hands and kissed Wiley, soft and gentle. "Test run," he murmured, and then kissed each corner of Wiley's lips. He pulled back and the door slammed behind him as he said, "Get some rest. You're gonna need it."

Wiley watched Holt stride down the path and disappear between the houses.

He stood with a hand on his mouth for a long time.

Chapter Two

"FIRST stop, get a move on." Kit slammed the car door closed and began striding away.

He was in his element, important planner mode, full of vision-this and imagine-that. For once, Holt was just along for the ride.

Holt got out and tugged Wiley with him to clamber out the same side. He hardly noticed the camera crew following, although he was very aware of Wiley's unfamiliarity with their presence, so he kept a loose hand circled around Wiley's wrist as they came around the car to join Kit. That made it easier for Wiley to hide from the cameras without it being obvious.

He'd decided since he got Wiley into this, he'd do what he could to make it as painless a process as possible. He squeezed again and Wiley looked at his hand, then quirked a smile at him.

Holt found his gaze lingering on the corner of Wiley's lips, the last place he kissed last night.

He let go so Wiley could explore and rolled his shoulders, surveying the sweeping lawns and manmade lake-and-fountain combo in the distance, and tried to stay neutral. He wouldn't choose a golf course for his wedding, but this wasn't exactly his wedding.

"Nope," Wiley said after returning to stand by him. "The clubhouse is all brass and glass and did I mention nope?"

Holt should push for more back-and-forth, maybe a more extreme negative take on the property that could be sliced into a sharp quip in edits. But he didn't want to needle Wiley, and he didn't want to pretend mild interest in the place. They'd only been here twenty minutes, but he gladly turned his back on the greens.

He slung an arm over Wiley's shoulders and started them trudging up the hill toward the parking lot.

"Good thing Kit is going to show us more options, because. Nope."

Wiley smiled. "So much nope."

"The next one will be better."

"And if it's not?"

Holt pulled Wiley tighter to him. "We'll decorate a garage if we have to, but it won't come to that. Kit has more to show us yet."

They would tour exactly two more possibilities, and most likely choose the final one, because the show worked in threes and from audience expectation. It was a go-to structure in the genre.

"Why am I getting the sense this one is a no? How can it be a no? Look at all that!" Kit stood at the top of the hill, hands on hips. He raised one to sweep over the manicured landscape. Then he took in their nope-faces and sighed. "Fine—I didn't think this would be it anyway. Too modern." He tugged the mini planner from the bag he kept over one arm and crossed the top item out with a flourish. "On to the next one."

Holt slowed his and Wiley's steps so Kit could walk ahead and talk to the camera crew on the way back to the car. He'd had their producer, Elaine, explain the live part of this episode. The whole thing was going to be shot and cut like a regular episode, but as a bonus and since it was one of their own getting married, a livestream would air at various points to have a more behind-the-scenes, intimate vibe. Elaine and Rick, camera guy and director, had worked up a quick guideline on how to minimize his and Wiley's exposure.

He'd explained it as wanting privacy and Wiley warming up to it after getting surprised by the proposal and being on the show. Since up until yesterday he'd been a steel trap about his private life, and they definitely caught that Wiley was currently overwhelmed but dealing, they accepted that. Which was convenient, since the foursome who schemed this into existence got together at Carla's for pregossip rush danishes and agreed they'd keep it a secret from everyone else.

"Am I right?" Kit's call trailed back to them.

Holt stopped beside the SUV and Kit in the driver's seat, waiting for them.

"Of course," Holt answered.

"You didn't even hear me." Kit rolled his eyes. "In your own little world for two again. I get it." He tutted, tucked his leg inside, and motioned, so Holt closed the door.

Holt and Wiley climbed into the middle seats and they jostled getting buckled and settled as the camera crew moved around them.

"I was reminding you of my Laws of Layering, which is the method to my planning madness and why we're doing this first. Start with the largest building block in your plan, and then add detail by smaller detail, until at the very end, it's but a sprinkle of glitter and grace to achieve perfection." Kit eyed them in the rearview mirror. "But if we don't pick the perfect venue, nothing else can go to plan."

"I know you have the perfect one to show us, and I'm excited to see everything, really. It's just that one was not it." Wiley glanced at Holt, seeming to seek an okay for saying that.

Holt casually reached over, laid his hand on Wiley's arm, and squeezed.

"We didn't even have to get out of the car, did we? We already knew." Holt winked at Wiley and laughed for the camera, but it was true. He'd sensed Wiley's dislike as much as he'd tried to hide his own.

Kit peppered them with questions, and Holt fielded most of them. Nothing too deep or personal, and nothing that could get them in trouble, but good quips and interplay for the stream and later edits. Wiley managed a few answers, and Holt found he laughed at most of them and smiled back easily when Wiley smiled at him.

If they stayed in sync like this, it would make things a whole lot easier.

They drove through the hilly countryside, and Kit pulled into a pick-your-own orchard. Holt, intrigued, sent Wiley a questioning look.

Wiley shrugged gamely and followed Kit's immediate exit from the car. Holt went with a bit less haste and joined them, edging between Kit and Wiley as Kit gave a brief on the property.

"There's the cute old farmhouse, the barn, a corral-thing with critters in it for background character, and acres of trees, some still with blooms."

"I bet it's pretty in the fall," Wiley said to Holt.

"I'm thinking so." Holt turned in a circle, liking the place and thinking Wiley did too. "This wasn't in business when we lived in Odalia, was it? I think Mom and Dad would have brought us here for wholesome, pretend-you-like-each-other-boys, family outing time."

"Ugh, outdoor activities, the worst." Kit flipped to a page in his planner, held up a finger, and then made a noise of satisfaction. "Established five years ago, Greenbrier Farms has apples, pears, soft fruit, tempting jams and baked goods made with each, and you can meet all their goats and geese and...." He waved a hand with a moue of distaste. "Such."

"Well, let's meet them." Wiley took hold of Holt's hand like it was natural and pulled him toward that background-character-making corral.

Holt grinned and set his sights on the spindly black-and-white goat pressed against the fence rail watching them.

"Hey, little guy," he said and tickled the goat's chin.

Wiley laughed and Holt couldn't keep from smiling as Wiley made instant friends with a squat pig.

"Have you ever been here?"

"No. I didn't get out much taking care of Grandma, and then.... Well." Wiley's jaw clenched, and he ducked lower to give the pig a sound belly rub. "You know."

Holt thought he was getting the idea. He knelt so they were closer and brushed dirt from Wiley's cheek. "I do." He glanced at the camera hovering and dropped his hand. "Do pigs purr? I think you're getting him to, at least."

Wiley seemed momentarily frozen, but then he grinned. "Possibly? Whatever he's doing, this porker is happy." He scritch-scratched on the pig's tummy and sides and then gave a sound pat before standing. "We should probably look into the barn and everything."

The pig grunted displeasure as Wiley walked away, and Holt laughed.

"I know how he feels," Holt teased.

Wiley blushed, and Holt fought the itch to touch that spot again.

"What an exactly-how-it-should-be barn." Wiley hurried into the barn and then stood at its center with his back to the camera. "So, we'd have the reception in here?"

"That's my thinking," Kit said from the huge open doors. "Wire chandeliers from the rafters, long tables so everyone sits family-style, toss some loose hay on the floor for atmosphere. But I'm spray painting the hay gold and wrapping the poles in gauze—bring a touch of glam to things."

"And the ceremony?" The words felt funny, and Holt avoided looking at Wiley.

"Honestly, I think the porch of the farmhouse. The inside is cute, but only the downstairs is available, as it's lived-in. Way better for a small holiday gathering or some such. At least then there'd be fresh hot cider." Kit circled both hands to shoo them along. He pivoted to frame the house. "You two on the porch framed by the woodworking, whatever attendants arrayed down the stairs, and everyone standing among the wildflowers. It'd have to be short and sweet for that, but I could make it work."

"I'm sure you could." Wiley let Kit lead him to the car.

Holt noticed the goat staring at them and went to give it a last pat.

"Well?" Kit motioned around as Holt joined them.

"It's definitely in the running. And better than the golf course." Wiley turned to Holt. "Agreed, my sweet?"

Holt swallowed a cough and his eyebrow shot up, more humor than warning. "I'm agreed."

"Hooray—we have a chance after all." Kit applauded. "Now, on we go. Remember, no firm thoughts or decisions until you've seen all three places."

As Kit pulled away, Holt caught Wiley waving goodbye to the animals.

Wiley shrugged but his chin went up an increment, so Holt leaned in.

"We'll have to see if the pig is available to be a groomsman." He watched Wiley fight a smile and lounged in the seat, unaccountably satisfied.

They traversed rural farms and fields and eventually got on the main—and these days, slow—highway leading into town.

"Third option, almost there." Kit turned between two river-stone pillars connected by a topiary archway. He stopped in the shadows and twisted to face them. "This time, reserve judgment for once we're out of the car."

"Can do," Holt agreed.

Kit speared Wiley with a look.

"Will do."

"Good. Because it's a glorious wonder. Not to influence you with my expertise, of course." Kit grinned. He eased off the brake and rolled the car to an opening in the hedges and trees to reveal an imposing Federal-style mansion in white, more river stone, and aproned by enormous porches to either side of its stark front door.

Kit parked a fair distance from the house and hopped out of the car. "It's better to see it on approach in the fresh air. Breathe it in—it's the Goldilocks outdoor venue—whiff of nature and freshness but not close-and-personal nature. If you know what I mean. Come on."

Wiley hesitated and glanced at Holt. Then he glanced at the camera and trotted after Kit to the center of the lush green lawn leading up to the grand home. When Holt got to them, he slid his hand into Wiley's and congratulated himself on not reacting when Wiley jumped at the contact.

"Behold. Sensational, am I right? Of course I am, don't answer." Kit threw back both arms and sucked in a deep breath. He pointed at the east wing porch and dragged that finger through the air across the home. "Vows on one side, pass through the house, reception and cake on the other. Fairy lights, an intimate quartet, yes. I can picture the whole grand affair. You?"

Holt nodded along. "We could have valet so guests get let off at the starting porch and then there's not a car logjam."

"Ever practical," Kit said tartly. "Wiley, tell me you're imagining more than parking logistics."

"Going a mile a minute here," Wiley said, meaningful only to Holt. "Can we see the backyard?"

"Yes, excellent suggestion. It's the hidden gem. This way." Kit slotted his elbow into Wiley's, tugged, and marched them toward the farther porch.

It forced Holt to let go of Wiley, but neither of them seemed to notice. He flexed his hand and frowned.

They stepped onto the porch, and Kit gesticulated and explained reception layout plans. Holt heard candles, copper bundles and rose-gold accents, ivory linen.

Wide stone stairs were cut into ivy and opened to an enormous oval stone patio backing into trees. Holt thought he could see the river down below.

Kit grabbed Wiley and started singing the notes to a familiar waltz, off-key and loudly and without shame. He spun Wiley away toward Holt and bowed.

Wiley bounced against Holt, so Holt sidestepped to catch and then stand behind Wiley, keeping his hands on Wiley's shoulders. His fingertips grazed Wiley's throat, slipping under Wiley's collar. He kept them there.

Kit moved to the center whorl of the huge stone pavers. "Sarah will do much, much better than I did."

Wiley reacted to the name. "Sarah Voss?"

"The very same." Kit began to smile.

"Owns the ballet and partner dance studio on Main Street, Sarah Voss?" Wiley clarified.

"Got it in one." Kit's eyes sparkled dangerously. "Oh, haven't I told you? That's your intimacy assignment from me—learning and performing a choreographed first dance. We'll go right to Sarah's after you make your venue choice. Isn't that exciting?"

Wiley's pulse fluttered and Holt glanced down. He couldn't tell if the reaction was excitement or dread.

His response was wholly dread, and he knew Kit would count on that.

Kit turned to the camera trailing him. "My dears watching along, I know you all know, but let's go over what I mean, in case you're newly tuning in." He *tsk*ed into the camera as if that was unbelievable. "Intimacy assignments are that little extra something every couple gets as a surprise from me, after I spend some time with them and think about their connection and needs. I don't want just a fabulous wedding—I want a marriage that'll be fabulous for the ages! So these are to get the couples to dig a bit deeper, maybe get a teensy bit stressed, and make them a whole lot closer by the time they say I do."

"Shall we dance?" Kit sashayed and hummed more of the waltz. "I won't tell you viewers what dance they'll learn—you'll have to wait and see! But anyone following our livestreams and social media peeks will get treated to a few spoilers and some of their rehearsals."

The camera found them for their reactions. If Holt's on-camera smile wasn't so practiced, he'd be grimacing.

Wiley, despite being pale under the tinge of a high flush, was holding together admirably well.

"Okay." Kit clapped. He went to and pushed at Holt and Wiley. "It's decision time." He turned back to the camera and monologued that the couple would go have a serious talk, go over the three amazing options he'd provided, and make their decision.

"That's our cue," Holt whispered to Wiley and guided him to one of the stone benches at the back of the patio terrace. He sat purposefully facing the dense woods and planted the heel of his hand at Wiley's opposite hip.

"Intimacy assignments in the episodes I watched were crafting a centerpiece for the couple's table or learning how to make fresh pasta or choosing items from the day spa menu to treat your affianced to." Wiley's pulse jumped again. "Dance? We have to learn a dance?"

"Let's just… deal with that later. I've learned it's best to deal with one thing at a time, and at the moment, it's time to choose the venue." Holt was impressed with how reasonable he sounded. "What do you think?"

Wiley repeated several inhale-and-exhale cycles and then nodded. "If it were for me, I think the farmhouse and goats and pig groomsman. But I think for the show this is way better."

"You'd be correct."

"Which did you like best?" When Wiley resituated so they could look at each other, his back pressed along the length of Holt's arm.

Holt hedged. "I'm happy with any of them." He also liked the farmhouse and goats best, but Wiley's instincts about wow factor and working easiest within the parameters of the show were dead-on.

"Liar. You hated the golf course as much as I did."

"How about I'm fine with any of them?" Holt tried. "But Wiley. It's immaterial."

Wiley caught on. "Ah, of course. It doesn't matter anyway since this is fake. We don't have to pick anything based on actual preference." He crossed his arms. "We're agreed here is indeed sensational, it'll be a fabulous fairy light dream, and Carla's cake will look amazing on the larger porch. I mean, there's a reason Kit brought us here last and called it every kind of perfect. And you know, big and fancy with copper and ivory linen accents might be fun. I don't go for fancy stuff—I should say, I never do anything fancy, that sounds better—I might as well for my wedding nonwedding."

Holt didn't go for fancy either but they were past that point. Wiley seemed past listening, but also, Wiley wasn't wrong. He tamped down unnecessary annoyance.

"It's not only that. Listen before you stomp off."

"Stomp off?"

"I don't mean that as anything. I just need you to listen before we have to be back on camera. I should have told you this before, but it got away from me." Holt sliced his hand through the air. "This is all going faster and more out of step than I intended. But look, this place has to be it. Kit booked it weeks ago."

"Oh." Wiley laughed hollowly. "Wow, sure. But of course, of course that's how it works and I'm an idiot."

"You're not."

"Liking the farm and the barn and the pig and thinking I had a choice? Feels a bit that way. At least it was genuine for the camera." Wiley took on a pleasantly neutral expression and started to stomp off. "Let's go tell Kit our decision."

Holt wanted to point out that was brand strategy, not a decision. That this wedding was Kit's harebrained idea and they were desperately working a rescue attempt. He lengthened his strides to follow Wiley and caught up easily, managing to get an arm around Wiley's shoulders as they got to Kit's anticipatory position at the end of the patio.

"And?" Kit clasped his hands under his chin and acted like he had no idea what they'd decide.

Wiley surprised Holt by answering for them.

"And you showed us some wonderful options, but as we talked about it, we realized there's no contest—it has to be here." Wiley smiled up at Holt. "But we're definitely going apple picking in the fall."

Holt rocked them side to side as if to agree and let his camera smile slide into place.

Kit fairly squealed with delight. "I knew this would be the one. It was made for you." He swept his arms around. "We'll do bare bulb strings of lights over the patio here, and guests will be free to come and go from inside. I'm thinking paper lanterns in the surrounding trees. All rose gold and white, of course."

Wiley nodded along. "Of course. That sounds, well, perfect."

"And it's just the start!" Kit launched at them and gave them a hug. "There's more to discuss and decide about the décor, but that's a different day's layering task. For the rest of today, well…. Come along, time to meet Sarah and your dancing fate."

"Do we really have to start that today?" Holt was ready to go to the hotel and decompress—off camera—so that was the last thing he wanted to hear.

Kit paused and planted a hand on his hip. "You're getting married in less than a month, darling brother. We should have started yesterday."

Wiley didn't grumble like Holt, but he did use Holt's momentary stillness to escape Holt's arm and walk with Kit to the car.

Holt grumbled deeper, mugged for the camera because this was something he was expected to want to do in the end, and retrained his focus. Day one and they were doing well. They had the venue sorted, and the rest should fall into place. A dance was merely another problem to tackle, figure out, and solve. Since that was his role on the show, he should be able to do it handily.

WILEY climbed the stairs to Sarah's dance studio and tried to decide if he could just not. He couldn't see any reason to learn a dance for a reception for a wedding that wasn't going to happen. Making decisions that were already decided was bad enough.

On the way here there wasn't any bringing that up to discuss with Kit because of Elaine and Rick. It would have been the best opportunity, as Kit was buoyant after the venue selection.

He sighed and pictured wildflowers, farmland, a happy pig, a relaxed Holt with that adorable goat and Holt taking the time to tell it goodbye.

But liking wildflowers wasn't the point. A dramatic, elegant, magazine-perfect setting for Kit to gild was. Wiley repeated that distinction the rest of the day. He should make it his mantra for getting through the rest of filming.

Wiley stopped and squished to the side at the top landing so the camera could stay with Kit. Holt stopped two stairs down, and Wiley should be annoyed Holt was still taller than him but…. No. Waves of body heat drenched him and he shivered.

"Sarah?" Kit called from the studio doorway and tiptoed inside.

As soon as the door was clear, Wiley rushed in after him. He shivered again, this time from a sudden chill.

The space was as he'd always pictured a dance studio should be, open with sunlight from the tall banks of windows at either end flooding the room and bouncing off the gleaming floor. Mirrors lined one long wall, and benches and cubbies lined the other.

"Welcome, welcome." Sarah stood tall in a black leotard, frothy skirt, legwarmers, and layers of scarves, her long silver hair in a tight bun. In her sixties, she was an institution in Odalia, teaching generations of little ballet prima-wannabes and nervous teens wanting to impress at prom.

Wiley had never been before—not like there was money for extras, and he'd never yearned to be the nutcracker prince or whatever—but he'd seen Sarah around town, and they'd chatted at some town events. He hoped she'd be merciful.

Kit was well into enthusing for the camera. "Everyone, say hello to the true diva of Odalia, Sarah Voss. A study in steely eleganza. Can you believe Sarah gave me my first comportment and movement lessons when I knew I was destined for performance? And here I am, back again—I love a full circle moment." He somehow made the introduction about him, but charmingly so.

He moved fluidly in relation to the camera and Sarah, positioning for the best angles and framing of what he wanted in the shot. Wiley had paid attention and jotted mental notes throughout the day for future reference.

After an explanatory conversation between Kit and Sarah about the dance and its purpose, Kit winked and headed for the door.

"Have fun, you two. We're not showing any dancing tonight, so we don't embarrass the lovebirds at their first lesson. See you tomorrow—décor and more, so get primed for monogram fonts and tablecloth colors and centerpiece containers. Good night from Odalia!" Kit waved and then halted without leaving. "Good?"

Rick gave a thumbs-up. "We've stopped recording and streaming." He wore a rig with a digital camera and a small cube webcam attached, which he constantly fiddled with. Wiley hadn't yet learned to tune it out.

"Great." Kit crossed back to Sarah. "Thanks for doing this, Sarah. It's so special that you agreed, and I know my dear gumdrops are in excellent hands."

Kit waved in their general direction and actually left.

Wiley inched closer to Holt and whispered, "Is that all, do you think?"

"I can only hope."

Holt sounded so pressed about it that Wiley bristled. Ridiculous, since he didn't want to dance either. But bristled.

Elaine sat on a bench and opened her show binder. "That's today's locations done. We have plenty of establishing and fill shots for the venue segment. I think…. Rick, let's just do a few staged here and we can call it a day. Since the dance needs to be a huge reveal at the wedding, we don't want to film much."

Wiley imagined the words *internal screaming* flashing on repeat. He and Holt would have to do this, at least to some extent, since Elaine and Rick and Sarah didn't know it was for show. For the show.

He did not deserve this. He should be making macaroni art canisters to hold the pens for signing the guestbook. He merited way more than learning a stupid dance they wouldn't even perform, given his whole volunteering to not torpedo the episode and make the show and Kit and Holt look absurd and cause a network and gossip meltdown.

Or it was exactly what he deserved for agreeing to this.

"We put ourselves at your mercy and expertise, Ms. Voss," Holt said with real charm.

"Miss Sarah. It's what all my students call me."

"Very good. Miss Sarah." Holt slid his hand into Wiley's and gave it a light shake. "I promise not to step on your toes any more than I can help it."

Wiley noticed Rick filming again. He looked down at Holt's hand in his and thought oh, right, and went with the impulse to go onto his toes and kiss Holt's cheek.

Holt's grip tightened almost painfully.

"Gee, thanks." Wiley grinned at Sarah. "He's such a real gentleman, always thinking of things like that."

Sarah smiled and pulled something up on her phone. "Kit and I agreed you both were best suited to a traditional partner dance. I've put together a playlist of options—see what you think. The music needs to be something that makes you *want* to dance."

Wiley accepted the phone and held it so he and Holt could read as he scrolled the titles. He lingered over one long enough before continuing to scroll for Holt to flip the screen back to that song.

"That would be a good pick—great song."

Wiley almost asked, *Really? As if you know it and like it too?* But he remembered they should know that about each other.

"Yeah?" Wiley angled his body so Holt obscured him from the camera. "What am I supposed to pick?" He burned with lingering resentment and humiliation from earlier.

Holt ran a hand up and down Wiley's arm. "Anything you like."

Wiley tilted his head. "Are you saying the song's not already in Kit's planner pack?"

"Yes. This was definitely not prearranged. I wouldn't have let Kit get away with it otherwise."

"You make a fair point. Dancing with me is probably the worst thing ever." Wiley nudged into Holt and smiled, moving so the camera could pick him up. "So yeah, I agree if you agree. But."

"But?"

"It's romantic but not a guaranteed happy ending. Maybe it isn't right for a wedding."

"It's right for our wedding." Holt smiled confidently. "That's our song."

"Yeah. Okay." Wiley didn't try to decipher it further and handed the phone to Sarah. "That was simple. It's nice how often we agree like that. You heard him. That's the one. It's on rotation at my house, so we've hummed our way through it a few times together. Which means we're not starting totally from scratch with it. And Holt's right: it's a great song we both like a lot."

That felt stupid and scripted, but it didn't seem to clang in the studio like it did in his head.

Sarah connected her phone to speakers and the slow, dreamy piano opening to "You Go To My Head" wafted through the studio. Wiley was pleased it was Billie Holiday, not Frank Sinatra's version, and he wondered what Holt thought about it.

"Billie's is always better," Holt whispered as Sarah maneuvered them into a standard dance frame.

"Also agreed," Wiley whispered back.

Holt's hand spread across his back and Wiley tried to relax, so he wound up standing even more awkwardly.

"I think you know one another quite well, so don't be so afraid of getting close." Sarah cupped one of her hands on each of their shoulders. "Closer," she urged and moved them a step, then two, then three inward.

Wiley's head fit under Holt's chin, and he heard Holt swallow.

Sarah patted Wiley's back and stepped away. "We'll work on choreography starting tomorrow. For now don't plan your steps, just move together and get a feeling for the music—for your song."

Wiley made an agreeing noise, or thought he did, but he couldn't tell. Muddled exhaustion swamped him. He'd barely slept last night, kept awake with his brain hard at it on the hamster wheel of overthinking everything the day might bring. Today had proved easier than he feared, but zipping place to place, and Kit's continuous stream of chatter, and trying not to mess up or give the pretense away was a lot. It wasn't like he was used to pretending anything on camera, much less being a besotted almost-married guy.

He forced that back and concentrated on the song and doing what Sarah suggested, and wound up doing a shuffle-sway. They continued the shuffle-sway, Holt adding a very slow turn, and Wiley stopped thinking about the ideal reaction and gave in to it.

"Yes, very good. I think that's enough for today."

Sarah's voice penetrated Wiley's awareness. She sounded distant and muffled. He huffed because he was warm and comfortable, and a second later his eyes shot open and he tensed.

Holt held Wiley incredibly close, Wiley basically napping against his chest, and their shuffle-sway had become a stand-in-place-and-barely-move sway. His belly quivered, and he caught a sigh before it could escape.

Wiley let out a long breath and leaned away. Holt shifted to hold his shoulders and stared down at him, jaw working and bright blue eyes dark with something that made Wiley want to burrow back in or bolt.

"Uhm." Wiley levered from Holt and summoned a grin. He didn't notice Holt's one-handed reach for him as he sighted the water cooler across the room and made for it as if he was dying of thirst.

He better not be.

Wiley gulped three paper cups of water and went in for another.

"Tomorrow, you said? What time?" Holt's voice carried to him, almost normal instead of thick and rumbly.

But traces of thick and rumbly remained. Wiley decided it was probably from talking all day and then not talking for the hours they danced. He checked the wall clock. Not even an hour.

"That was super sweet, guys. We're gonna have some good footage from that." Elaine pulled Holt to the windows overlooking Main Street. "Rick and I want some silhouetting—Wiley? Can you join us, please?"

Wiley crushed the paper cup and tossed it in the trash as he joined them.

"Sarah?" Elaine motioned, and the song started playing again. She nodded and got out of Rick's way.

Wiley didn't close his eyes, too aware of the camera for that. Too aware of Holt. But he dutifully shuffled to the music and let Holt spin them around.

"Okay, great. Thanks, guys." Rick fiddled with the camera and went to show Elaine the playback.

"You'll have Holt and Wiley to yourselves for tomorrow's session, Sarah. We'll be out with Kit getting some pickups and establishing stuff." Elaine clapped her binder shut. "And that's it—at least for you all. Rick and

I are off to find Kit and see how the intros and explainers are going. Good job, everybody. Thanks again, Sarah."

Sarah bowed graciously, and Rick followed Elaine down the stairs.

"Is nine too late?" Sarah looked to Holt and then Wiley. "I'd make it earlier if I could, but I have long-scheduled classes I don't want to cancel. This is exciting, but that's not exactly fair to my students."

"Then see you at nine, Miss Sarah." Holt turned to Wiley. "Sound okay to you?"

"Not a problem. We agree more than we disagree. Lucky, right?" Wiley smiled at Sarah.

He was smiling more—for, at, fake, in reaction, weak attempts—than he had the entire year until now.

"Very. And a bit of wedding jitters as well." Sarah gripped their arms and led them to the door. "You're doing a very good job of hiding it, don't worry. I've just been around a while."

"Don't tell anyone you're onto us," Holt teased.

"You're safe with me. See you tomorrow." Sarah stood on the landing and watched them go. "Your homework for tonight is to get some rest."

"That won't be a problem," Wiley muttered as they stepped onto the sidewalk.

A nondescript car was parked at the curb waiting for them. Holt held open the back door and slid in after Wiley.

"Has this wrung you out already?"

Wiley scooched all the way over until he was against the other door. He pressed two fingers to his forehead and then frowned at them. "I'm in full can't-wait-to-get-home-scrub-this-makeup-off-and-get-into-bed mode, and I offer no apology for that." He flopped back in the seat. "And it's only day one."

"That makes our third agreement." Holt's legs were so long his bent knee grazed Wiley's thigh. "You're doing really well, and you're definitely allowed to be tired."

"Fourth." Wiley watched a familiar route go by and didn't question how the driver knew where he lived. "We agreed about the venue, so that's four." He didn't mask the tartness that crept into his tone.

"I suppose we did." Holt drummed his fingers and started to get out as they pulled up to Wiley's house.

"No, don't. We're both tired." Wiley leaned in so he could lower his voice. "I can get inside by myself and, well. I'm ready for that. No offense."

"None taken. Is quarter of six good? Should I get you at the bakery?" Holt paused. "Are you a morning person?"

The third question seemed out of nowhere, but Wiley readily answered each. "Yes, do, yes, that's fine, and yes, I am. Although a morning person usually not in the middle of filming a staged reality show." Wiley popped the door open. "Thank you," he said to the driver. "Well. Good night."

Holt blinked slowly and moved incrementally forward but then sat back. "Good night, Wiley. Get some rest."

The car remained until he had unlocked the front door, turned on a light, and waved.

Wiley scrubbed clean in the shower, ate an assembly of food that didn't have to be cooked for dinner, and face-planted in bed.

He lay there telling himself to prepare for tomorrow. Think about camera angles, organic reactions, readiness to keep smiling. Instead he remembered Holt's spicy, musky cologne and kinda sorta wished he'd let Holt walk him inside.

Chapter Three

OH, *I Do!*

Well, well, well. Who saw that one coming?

No one! That's who, and if anyone tries to claim otherwise, call them out as the shameless liar they are (y'all know I live in the comments and y'all know I'll check you—everybody's on notice—even I'm not pretending I had even a whiff of this).

Our dear Mr. Fix-it is getting hitched! I had no clue he was dating—has he ever dated? remind me if I'm forgetting someone—much less getting this serious. Still waters and dark horses and all, hmmm?

At first I was disappointed it wasn't Kit's HEA reveal—gather around me for comfort, Kittens—but now that it's gotten out what Kit's slime of an ex was up to (many, many up-tos who were not Kit, and Kit

trying to keep a lid on that and their dignity, bless), I'm
thrilled he scraped off that slime, emerged tanned and
glorious from a deserved Maui refresh, and decided to
turn that negativity into a big positive for big brother.

What a sweetie. As we've said from the start.
Here's to rising above.

I've always been up front that I'm no Holster, but
he looked genuinely moved at Wiley Grey's (whose?!)
acceptance and whew, that strong protective arm around
Wiley getting back to the bus…. Can you say *fans self*?
Holt's a strapping 6'4" and his boo could fit in his pocket!
I'm a sucker for that and not ashamed to admit it.

I also might be a sucker for small-town hometown
torches getting rekindled. Especially when they involve
adorbs auburn-haired elves who can apparently design,
draw, and bake, and swoon-worthy beaus who can
swoop in and sweep clear the dark clouds and let the
light of l-o-v-e shine.

But I'd never admit that aloud.

What do you all think? Is Wiley deserving of Holt?
(Do we know enough yet to say? Of course not, but
we're here to judge, not to be reasonable!) Will Wiley
want to get married in a barn or something equally
small-town charming as heck? Will Holt have to last-
minute throw together centerpieces and construct bench
seating from old wine barrels and a trellis from sticks
and save his own wedding day?

Tell me your thoughts, Kittens & Holsters. I'm
gasping here.

As always: Claws out and drills drawn, let's get
into it in the comments!

WILEY wrapped his hands around the coffee mug
Carla set next to him but didn't lift his head from the

counter. The warmth penetrated his fingers and scalp and calmed some of the throbbing from another night of restlessness.

"It's not too late to back out." Carla patted his back. "That's a lie. It's really super too late to back out, but I'll help you escape to Canada if you want."

"Thanks." Wiley sat up enough to hold his face over the steaming coffee. "You're a true friend."

Carla slid a danish to him.

"And you feel guilty for urging me to agree to this."

Carla slid a plate of mini muffins closer to join the danish.

"I'll be fine. There's no reason I shouldn't be fine." Wiley took a huge gulp of coffee and sighed as it spread through him. "There's also even less acting to do than I first thought."

"How's that?"

"Almost everything is already planned, chosen, booked—done and done. I just have to pretend like I'm trying to make tough choices and then go with what Kit wanted all along." Wiley drank the rest of his cup down to chase the bitter, lingering humiliation away.

It wasn't important.

"Wow. That's kind of a bummer. I always guessed some of these reality shows had to be set up beforehand or else they couldn't do what they do. But—everything?"

Wiley shrugged. "Effectively. I think there's always something preset for all the episodes we've watched with couples bickering over crepe paper roses or baby's breath sprigs, rose trellises or a grotto spring. It makes logistical sense. This one it's doubly such. Remember, it was supposed to be Kit's wedding."

"Hmm, true." Carla pulled a face. "His and your tastes are nothing alike. You're going to be forced to marry in clouds of fairy lights and golden fringe and frou-frou, aren't you?"

"An unexpected bonus to that I'm-not-actually-getting-married part of things."

Carla ripped Wiley's danish in half and chewed it thoughtfully. "He better let you choose something. Even if it is make-believe, the groom-to-be should be entitled to some say-so."

The song from their dance wove through Wiley's mind, and it was too easy to summon the feeling of being in Holt's arms.

"Wiley, what is that?"

"What?" Wiley's eyes snapped open.

"That."

Wiley tilted his head. "I need more than *that*, that."

Carla grinned. "You're blushing. Whew." She held the back of her hand to his cheek and then fanned herself. "A scorcher."

"I'm not. I'm tired. You know I run warm when I'm tired."

"Sure. That seems legit." She eyed him. "Hotter than you ever blushed mooning over Kit. Just saying."

Wiley hadn't thought about Kit to blush over since spying the tacky show tour bus in the park. He was too busy and distracted.

"I'm not gonna let this drop. You better tell me before they get here."

"Tell you what before we get here?" Kit asked from the kitchen door. He grinned. "Good morning. Almost time to get a move on. Hope you're ready. But first, yes, yes. Do tell."

Wiley glared at Carla, who smiled serenely.

Holt stood behind Kit and studied Wiley. He pushed Kit forward and squeezed past, making the wide rustic doorway seem small, and came around the counter to slide onto a stool by Wiley. "Everything okay?"

"Yes. I was only saying I didn't sleep great last night, so I'll try not to be in a total brain fog today." Wiley shouldn't let his leg relax so it firmly touched Holt's, but he did. "It's no big deal, though."

"Blushing," Carla mouthed at him as she filled two more mugs.

"Thank you." Holt had a long drink. "That feels good. You make good coffee, Carla."

She pushed her hands up and teased, "I know. And help yourself to any goodies you want."

"Tragically, just black coffee for me, dear. These pants would never forgive me for even a bite of anything." Kit smoothed his palms down the very slim slim-cut fit of his light blue dress pants.

"No such tragedy here." Holt waggled his eyebrows and ate a danish in one huge bite. He swallowed it with alarming speed and then leaned on his elbow closer to Wiley. "Let us know when you need a break today. There's plenty of time for several, it's going to be a long day, and you have to pace yourself."

Wiley nodded.

"I mean it. Yeah?" Holt pressed.

"Yeah, sounds good." Wiley could tell Holt was genuine and smiled over finishing his breakfast.

"Are we ready, then?" Kit asked as he left without waiting for an answer.

Holt started to gather the dishes, but Carla waved him off.

"I'm good, thanks. And about to open so my part-timer should be here by now." She shooed them along.

"Have a great day! Film amazing things! Be the star I know you to be."

"You have a great day too, Carla. Thank you for the coffee." Holt somehow got his arm around Wiley and ushered them past the back of the counter area toward the kitchen.

Carla whispered to Wiley as he walked past, "Blush. Ing." She poked his side and snickered, and then she hustled the other direction to raise the shades and open the front door.

Wiley couldn't grumble or catch a quick nap as they got in the car. Elaine and Rick waited for them, Rick in the passenger seat, Elaine on the back bench with her binder open and fingers busy on her phone. He greeted them and everyone got settled, and then Rick motioned he'd started filming.

"Day two! I can't wait to get started. With our dream of a venue realized, now it's time to set the mood," Kit enthused. He eased the car from the back parking area of Carla's bakery and went around the block to Main Street. "We're so fortunate the venue is available for us to camp out and be 'in situ' while we build the next layer of Holt and Wiley's wedding fantasy."

Wiley watched the town stream past and tried to appear interested. When they arrived, Rick stopped filming, and they all got out of the car. Wiley stood and waited for whatever cue, but Elaine, Kit, and Rick went off, deep in discussion about shots and framing and the best light on the best porch for them to finish the setup.

"Want to have a walk around?" Holt glanced at the three gesturing and blocking scenarios on the larger porch where the reception would be. "They'll be a while."

"But we are filming today?"

Holt shook his head and looped an arm around Wiley. "I'm not doing great with this, I'm sorry. Normally, couples get production notes and schedules and such so they know what to expect during filming. Not so much that there's zero spontaneity, but plenty to keep them from feeling out to sea as we put them through the process. We don't have a write-up for this episode or I'd give you one."

"Ah." Wiley was relieved more than anything. Not being filmed or having to be at the ready at every moment was fine by him. "So then tell me. The gist."

Holt's thumb brushed his nape and he shivered.

"I wonder if this chill will hold until our… final day of not actually doing this." Holt tightened his hold and basically tucked Wiley into his quilted flannel shirt.

Wiley held in a moan of appreciation, but he did let himself smoosh closer in.

"I like it. I've always enjoyed the cool weather of early spring and late fall the most." Wiley motioned toward the rolling valley beyond the lawns. "There's fog, a reason to cozy into layers or your house with cocoa, but you're not held prisoner there by brutal heat death or brutal cold worse than death. Fall is my absolute favorite. There's just something about a crisp, drizzly day and a fire crackling inside and the world colorful but muted."

Holt tightened his hold even more. "I always wanted to get married in the fall. If I got married. It's my favorite season as well."

"Oh." Wiley didn't know what else to say to those many implications. "You were going to give me the gist?"

"Right. I definitely was." Holt cleared his throat. "I'll find out particulars on what the livestream changes, but essentially we have brief bursts of filming with a lot of waiting around each day. And we'll have some days we don't film at all in the next few weeks, depending on availability, weather, that sort of thing. I'll bring a daysheet to the bakery every morning we film, and that will fill you in on that day's shooting plans."

"Sounds good." Wiley glanced toward the house as they got farther away across the wide lawn. "What are we filming today?"

Holt fished a piece of paper from his left cargo pocket and unfolded it one-handed. Wiley took it, scanned it, and understood enough to get they were going to be here all day and he'd be expected to do very little during it.

"What do we do on the days we don't film?"

"You know, that's a good question." Holt laughed. "Ordinarily I'm busy making things, or fixing things, or helping the crew make or fix things. I haven't ever had to think about it."

"Well. We can figure that out together." Wiley looked up and smiled. "I'm sure we can find something worthwhile. That isn't dancing."

Holt stopped their lazy stroll and turned into Wiley. He smiled back, all eye crinkles and softened gaze, and ran a knuckle up Wiley's jaw.

"I'm certain of it," Holt whispered, and tilted his hand to cup Wiley's head as he lowered for a kiss.

Wiley closed his eyes and breathed out as Holt kissed his cheek, the bridge and then tip of his nose, and he held his breath as Holt's mouth opened over his, warm and firm. He rolled forward when Holt moved back and Holt rumbled with quiet laughter, braced the other hand on his hip, and nibbled Wiley's lower lip.

Holt bit harder—just enough to steal the drowsiness from Wiley's limbs—and curled his tongue into Wiley's mouth.

Wiley did moan at that, long and low, as his hands crept up under Holt's jacket to splay on Holt's chest.

He imagined all the muscle he felt jumping under his touch and went cold-hot. Wiley let one hand explore, fingers trailing down Holt's side and ribs, until he pressed his palm to Holt's back.

Holt dug in harder—hands, their stance, lips—and deepened the kiss.

All Wiley could think about was how good it felt, how good they fit. He wanted to tumble them onto the lush grass. He wanted to hear Holt grunt again. He caught Holt's tongue between his teeth and gently held it as he rubbed circles over Holt's chest and back.

Their kiss broke and it took a bit to register that Holt had gone rigid and still. Wiley opened his eyes and peered up.

Holt's mouth was compressed and the hands that moments ago had held him so completely were locked on his shoulders, but after a beat Holt smiled and kissed Wiley's forehead.

Movement caught Wiley's attention, and he noticed Rick. Filming them. With Elaine behind, tapping her binder and motioning them over.

Disappointment, confusion, embarrassment all doused Wiley back to cold reality.

He nodded and mumbled, "Ah, good thinking. I see."

Holt seemed to parse that, and then his smile broadened. "Ready?"

Wiley didn't withdraw from Holt's arm as they turned and walked to the house, but the warmth was gone. Of course that was because they were being filmed and it was for the audience. Of course the kiss didn't mean anything. Of course the kiss shouldn't mean anything.

"We're offline," Rick said as they approached.

"Gorgeous shot. You two are nicely matched." Elaine ushered them along. "And adorable."

"Aw, thanks, Elaine." Holt loosened his hold on Wiley and called as he strode toward the SUV, "Getting my water, only be a minute."

Wiley climbed onto the porch and determinedly put the kiss and everything else out of his mind.

"There you are. Sit here." Kit swept across the deck from inside the house and pointed Wiley into a chair pulled out from a huge round wood-plank table.

Holt sat in the one to Wiley's left, with Kit diagonal from them. To Wiley's right was a camera that could get all three in the frame. Lights and props were arrayed around the table, and crew members Wiley had yet to meet milled busily in the background.

"Rick's going to be mobile, working on candid reactions and livestream content. So don't worry about trying to keep track of him. And pretend like this," Elaine said while planting both hands on the camera, "isn't here."

"I'll do my best." The empty table offered no clues, so Wiley added, "With what? What layer are we choosing today?"

"Décor. Things like centerpieces and place settings and little guest gifts that will act as seating cards." Kit shrugged. "The usual."

As if Wiley knew the ins and outs of what the usual meant. He turned to Holt. "Which things am I supposed to choose?"

Holt's eyebrows arched but then he hummed thoughtfully. "I think it'll be apparent. But don't worry, we won't film it in one go, so you won't be continually on the spot to choose what's behind door number one or door number three."

"That's good, since I always go with two."

They didn't share any humor. As Elaine called for quiet on set, Wiley watched Holt's expression adjust into a pleasant mask and he tried to do the same. He repeated his mantra and tried some deep breathing, and then he focused on the task at hand.

The following hours were a flurry of napkins, how to fold and present the napkins, napkin rings or no napkin rings, matching the napkins to the tablecloths or contrasting, and if napkin rings, whether or not to match them to the dinnerware.

He nodded at wineglasses and champagne flutes and hand-blown water glasses. Beautiful, rustic, elegant shapes, each unique, so every guest will feel special using them, Kit gushed. He flipped through embossed paper or little figurines or tiny slates for name cards on the tables. He hefted the weight of various chargers in various metallic shades. Remember, rose gold will always land somewhere between too much and perfection, Kit praised.

Wiley paid extra attention to the items Kit showed them with extra flair, but found he paid the most attention to Holt's reactions.

By the end, he and Holt were surrounded by a fort built from sample books and rings of materials and stacked plates.

"I think that should give our couple plenty to think about, don't you?" Kit made eyes at the camera. There was no fort built to hide any of him. He reached for a vase, the dark pink globe dripping gold from the top, with inserts for flowers, and tossed it into his other hand to contemplate. After a moment he snapped his fingers. "Wiley, Wiley, I have it! Remember those dear and so-awful kitschy little village houses your granny collected?"

Wiley looked away from the vase—actually for-real awful and what he knew Kit wanted him to choose—and nodded. He remembered easily. Grandma owned several when he'd moved in with her full-time at six years old, and he'd given her one every Christmas they shared thereafter. She loved them.

"Oh my gosh—we should find some to use as centerpieces! It's too perfect. The place cards can tell people to go to the inn or the mill or whatever." Kit grinned. "What do you think?"

"I think that's…." Wiley glanced at Holt, who sat stone-faced, staring at the so-very-awful pink vase. "Great. It would mean a lot to me." He genuinely liked the idea and really hated how it came about. He cleared his throat. "And we don't have to find any. We can use mine."

Kit's eyes got comically huge. "What? You still have them? And Granny's been gone what…. Well, a while at least."

Wiley shifted uncomfortably and nodded. He kept them because they belonged in the house, displayed on the shelves he remembered Holt had hung over the living room windows for that exact purpose, and he didn't know what else to do with them. He might love them a bit too.

"That's so sweet." Kit leaned close and patted Wiley's arm. "You've just always been the sweetest."

It wasn't quite cutting, but it wasn't quite kind. It was how Kit had always been.

"That's Wiley—sweet but never saccharine. Sentimental but not syrupy. One among the many things about him I cherish." Holt covered Wiley's hand with his where Wiley picked at a loose thread on a fabric sample. "There's more than enough buildings for the tables. We'll choose our favorites and the place cards can be made to match."

"Oh, fantastic." Kit's gaze angled briefly but he set the vase down. "They'll go with everything I've shown you, so don't let that worry you as you decide on all the rest. I bet we can figure out a way to get flowers into those dear little houses and huts and such."

Filming cut, and Janet called lunch was ready.

Wiley's stomach gurgled. His predawn danish had deserted him hours ago.

He didn't wait for Kit to add any rejoinder about the village set or for Holt to join him. It was a small act of independence, but it still felt good to just get up and walk to the back patio where craft services had set up.

"No sushi, but the rolls are amazing. Which is a problem since I'm off carbs." Elaine eyed the basket of Carla's amazing yeast rolls and put two on her plate. "At least I will be when we're done with this shoot."

"They're good for you, I promise." Wiley took a bite of one. "I have to think carbs are the perfect food for long days on set and longer days keeping everything in order. Filling, delicious, all that quick energy."

"You make a sound argument." Elaine grabbed two more rolls. "Very sound." She nibbled one and then said, "This shoot is different from our usual. Harder, but in a good way."

"Oh?"

"We're doing a lot of it on the fly, because Kit wouldn't breathe a word of what the big secret reveal was, even to me or production. And we're in charge of planning episodes—before we film them." She laughed. "At first we were very annoyed by all the mystery and then having to scramble and get things together, but it's actually fun. I haven't worked like this since film school days when we made terrible artsy shorts on shoestring budgets. Which, to be fair, still isn't like that—it's not like we don't have the formula down and a good budget to meet it. But yeah, fun."

"Couldn't you have asked Holt?" Wiley ate another roll.

"He doesn't breathe a word, period. But then you know that." Elaine pushed at Wiley's shoulder. "No, that's not true. You're clearly the only person he tells everything to. It's super cute. Everyone just loves you, and everyone agrees the two of you together are super cute."

Wiley didn't contradict or correct her. He couldn't—and he didn't want to.

"We had a pool going. Most of us bet on the announcement being about or for Kit. Rick and Jerry—he helps in carpentry, have you met? Anyway, Rick and Jerry bet on Holt, mostly to be contrary, and came up huge." Elaine pulled a face. "Uh, no disrespect."

"None taken. I get it."

Elaine smiled. "We haven't bet on anything since that, and everyone thinks you're great. And a much better match for Holt than Kit, as if that was ever in question."

"Yes, as if." Wiley laughed lightly. "Well. I'm glad to hear all that. Including Rick and Jerry coming up the big winners."

"I'll be sure to tell them." Elaine hovered over the rolls and then nabbed one more. "Since I can say I'm carbo-loading now, it's silly not to have another."

"Take three," Wiley teased, and kept up a friendly grin until she'd grabbed a bottle of water and walked away.

He filled a plate with an assortment of fruit and veg and wraps and more rolls, and thought about the crew gossiping and deciding he was good people. Good people who made a perfect match with Holt.

Wiley escaped the food table before anyone else could strike up a conversation, retreated to the opposite side of the patio, and tucked into the stone niche at the far end, well away from the tables with people coming and going from them. He sipped coffee and then opened a sparkling water, wondering how he could get so dehydrated simply sitting in place.

Must be the lights.

"You were supposed to say that was a lovely, sentimental idea, but the pink vase was better." Holt nodded at the bit of room next to Wiley, and when Wiley didn't protest, he lowered into it.

They made a tight fit, and Holt took up two-thirds of the niche, even sitting diagonally with his legs outstretched. Wiley sat up straighter and pulled his legs in—otherwise they'd cross Holt's—and noticed without wanting to how warm and hard Holt's thigh and bicep were pressed into his.

Holt didn't start eating but also didn't say anything more. When Wiley checked, he stopped with a grape midbite in his front teeth. Holt seemed placid as ever, but something Wiley thought might be anger sparked in his eyes.

"I know. Sorry." Wiley dropped the grape and wiped his hand on his pants. "It just took me off guard. It's not like we can't say we changed our minds and go with the Snoballs. Uh, vases."

"We could but we won't. Kit doesn't need to get his way with everything. Production hasn't purchased anything in quantity yet, and it is *our* wedding." Holt quirked a smile and then looked away. "I'm who's sorry."

"Sorry?" Wiley shook his head. "Why?"

Holt let out an impatient breath. "Kit being so Kit about the village."

"Oh." Wiley didn't think other people really noticed how very Kit that Kit could be at times. At all times. It was nice to learn Holt did and that instance bothered Holt, for whatever reason. "It's fine. I know how he is."

"Sure. And same. But that's not really an excuse."

Wiley shrugged. Suddenly it didn't matter that Kit thought the village was kitschy and awful and he'd made the wrong not-pink choice. "Thank you. But it really is fine. I'm fine, and we get to pick houses together. Which I think is something almost-nonmarried married people do."

"I'm certain it's in the handbook. And genuinely liking and looking forward to picking the small houses with your not-fiancé has just been added."

A bubble of happiness rose up through Wiley, and he let it out with a laugh.

Holt grinned, ate a roll in one huge bite, and then swallowed hard. He glanced about and then said thickly, "May I?" Holt pointed at Wiley's water. "I forgot to grab anything."

"Yeah, of course."

Wiley watched Holt drink his sparkling water. The sinuous motion of Holt's throat. The way Holt's hand engulfed the can. The drops of moisture left on Holt's lips and thumb.

Then, like a weirdo, when Holt handed the can back, he had an immediate drink and definitely didn't dwell on the ghost of warmth in the metal or anything like that.

"You can come over today before our dance lesson. Unless you have something else to do."

Holt ate another roll and Wiley gave him the water.

"Keep it, I have coffee. Anyway, then it's decided immediately, and we can move on to other wedding-but-not-getting-married stuff."

"Good thinking." Holt drained the water and looked longingly at Wiley's coffee mug.

Wiley handed it over.

"Thanks." Holt had a long drink and sighed. "The big production storage shed is being moved to the grounds today, but no need to risk Grandma's village until the night before the ceremony. I'll take pictures and make a list, which will be more than enough for Kit and the printers to work from."

"I'm good with that plan." Wiley ate more grapes, since he hadn't planned on needing a third beverage. "Oh, but what about flowers?"

"I'll measure everything tonight, and the florist can make arrangements in small vases or containers. Not all the houses have openings that I recall, so it makes the most sense to keep those separate."

"Will the florist offer gold roses?"

Holt laughingly rolled his eyes. "Lord, I hope not." He lifted the coffee mug to finish it, paused, and tipped it toward Wiley. "Do you want the rest? I should go get you another."

Wiley smiled and shook his head. "No, I'm fine. Thanks."

"You're very nice about letting me steal your drinks, thank you. I will go get more, though, hold on." Holt shifted and had to get very much into Wiley's space to maneuver from the bench. He stopped, weight balanced on a palm against the bench, and blinked at Wiley. His gaze dropped to Wiley's mouth before dragging back up. Holt's eyes softened and his lips went slack as he inched forward.

Wiley parted his lips in anticipation, certain Holt was thinking about kissing him and wanted to kiss him and was about to kiss him.

Wiley wanted Holt to kiss him.

"Guys? We need you back on set."

Holt cursed under his breath, and Wiley startled to peer over Holt's shoulder and see Elaine motioning them along.

Rick wasn't there. At least he couldn't immediately find Rick. So, no camera. So… what?

So he couldn't overthink it.

Wiley let go of Holt's thigh—he didn't realize he'd grabbed hold of it—as Holt stood. He carefully stacked his dishes and the empty can and barely wobbled as he got to his feet and straightened into Holt's waiting frame. Holt walked them past craft services and back to the table no longer arrayed with a fortress of décor options.

Wiley smiled blandly at Kit, who regarded them with a touch of speculation. He didn't look directly at Holt but didn't avoid doing such.

"What's up?" he asked.

"We're going to finish with the discussion for decisions on décor. And then we're doing a walkthrough of the house to have some filler reaction shots for our first day segment." Elaine had her binder open on the table and her hands on her thighs as she read over it. "It helps you haven't seen in there yet, but just act like it's all brand-new and undecided, okay? After that we'll need Kit, but you two are done."

As Kit settled, Wiley noticed how everything they'd been shown was reorganized into two piles on the table behind Kit. One pile obviously the "these are so perfect" they were expected to opt for and the other obviously what they should call "these are pretty but not for us."

"Let's have Kit guide us through your choices. And then we'll do set backup and have you two sort into yes, maybe, and definite no." Elaine moved her binder to a different table. "Sound good and clear?"

"Wonderful, my best Lainey-Loo." Kit quickly went over each item, and then sat forward in his chair to do a series of breathing exercises he'd explained helped him relax and set his core for projecting.

Makeup fluttered in and touched up Wiley's natural no-makeup look, and he assumed an attentive posture. Blobs of people past the halo of the lights moved in the background, and Rick got set to film. Wiley glanced at Holt, who was checking something on his phone.

"All right, everyone, quiet please." Elaine backed up two paces and made eye contact with each of them. "Ready?" She dropped the slate and then counted down from five and pointed at Kit.

"After a tough but resolute deliberation, because who wouldn't be tempted by each and every little thing I showed them, Holt and Wiley have made their choices." Kit scooped up the items and transferred them to the table between them. "This layer is going to be a divine mixing of textures and patterns, all held together with gold accents and rose undertones."

Wiley zoned out as Kit described the materials and their attributes as he unfurled a length of fabric that would be the tablecloth, folded a napkin into a napkin ring, and set one of the hand-blown glasses next to a salad plate.

"What made you want these dishes? This pattern?" Kit speared him with a look and waited for an answer.

Wiley really studied them for the first time and improvised. "The others were pretty but… busy. These are so simple but eye-catching, with the double band of gold on an otherwise plain-seeming bisque. It reminded us of the rings we picked out. And the weighty china has such a tangible, satisfying heft."

Holt shifted next to him and Kit's eyes went wide, but then Kit grinned and reached over to squeeze Wiley's arm.

"Oh, that's good. That's so good." Kit waved a hand in front of his face. "I love when design details join personal context to become so meaningful."

"We're super pleased too." Wiley leaned and touched his shoulder to Holt's in an affectionate bump.

"As happy with these as the plates?" Kit held up a fork. "Holt? Why these? And tell us just a little bit more than something practical."

Holt plucked the matching knife from the set—handles forged to resemble rustic cut branches in a low-toned rose gold—and balanced it in his palm. "As you know, I love hiking and camping and getting into nature whenever possible. I've worked at convincing Wiley to join me ever since we started dating, and when he at last agreed, well…. Those were the best hikes of my life." He shrugged artlessly and smiled at Wiley. "So far."

"He makes it sound like a protracted campaign, but it didn't take that long." Wiley rolled his eyes. "I mean. I like walking and outside, and walking outside."

"The hikes, sure. The camping...." Holt *tsk*ed sadly. "The few times you've deigned to camp, you still insist we need an air mattress."

"Yes, because I'm absolutely in the right and we absolutely do. I'm certain your viewers would back me up on that if you had an online poll." Wiley managed to laugh and skip past thinking about being in a tiny tent in the middle of nowhere wrapped in a blanket burrito with Holt. He said to Kit, "Okay, so I'll admit I'm not a natural at being a back-to-nature guy. But Holt has shown me a lot of the positives to be had out there. In the woods. Doing woodsy stuff."

"Oh, I'm sure. I'm very sure." Kit waggled his eyebrows and the fork at the camera. "Ahem. Moving on."

Wiley smiled until he thought his face would crack as they continued the tablescape tour. He chuckled when Kit offered witticisms, pulled together sincere enough answers that didn't seem trite or practiced, and looked adoringly at Holt when Holt was asked to comment on the wineglasses and centerpiece mats.

"All right, that does it for us here." Elaine gestured for them to get up and follow her. "We'll get those interior reactions, and then you boys are dismissed."

Wiley didn't have to pretend being impressed for the interior reactions. The house was spacious and grand, and displayed wealth it had the better taste not to outright flaunt in every aspect, from the handmade tile floors to the cashmere pillows on the foyer settees and gleaming beveled glass french doors.

Less easy was pretending he didn't know what they'd discussed in the past two days, avoiding that in their real-but-fake conversation, and that he wasn't preoccupied by thoughts of cozy fires and cozier starry nights on the camping excursion Holt had said would be perfect and romantic.

"Wiley, what do you think of this space for you and your attendants?" Kit thrust open a set of huge double doors to reveal a morning room in blue and white. "We'll bring in a full-length mirror and little dressing table, but otherwise it should be so suitable. Hm?"

It struck Wiley he had no attendants. Or could reasonably ask anyone to be such even if he wanted to, considering the wedding was a sham. He blinked and cast about for an answer he couldn't find.

"You can use this room for getting ready. But Kit—we discussed this—we aren't having attendants. Despite the rose-gold sparkle, your flair, and this house, Wiley and I decided on relatively simple overall. Remember?" Holt pulled Wiley to him under an arm and smiled. His voice had an edge.

Kit put a hand to his forehead. "I'm getting carried away! Imagining Wiley with an army of gorgeous guys and gals in dusky-rose taupe and seeing stars. Of course, of course. Allow me to rephrase. Wiley, would you like to shimmy into your tux here the morning of?"

"I wouldn't hate it," Wiley said lightly. "You know me, and you picked the room to prove it. This beautiful room will give me a magical start to the day."

The room was beautiful. Way fussier and filled than Wiley cared for but beautiful with a distinguished, regal charm nonetheless. Since he wouldn't be here again or in a tux, it didn't much matter, so it was easy to agree.

"Wonderful! Now, Holt. For you." Kit swept out of the room.

Holt held Wiley back long enough to make eye contact, plant a kiss on his temple, and murmur something he couldn't quite hear.

"Okay, that's cut. Thanks, everyone." Elaine jotted notes as she spoke. "Holt, we already toured your ready room. And that's all the interiors we need to see." She pointed at them. "You two are dismissed! Remember, we're not filming with you tomorrow. Get some rest and see you at five the next day."

"This is nice. I could get used to not having to be on set day in, day out." Holt kept hold of Wiley as they walked through the foyer and massive front door and down the stairs into the surrounding landscape garden.

"Don't get too used to it." Elaine narrowed her eyes. "Although…." She trailed off and then shrugged. "Anyway, see you soon enough, but believe me, I'll text if there's a fix-it emergency."

Holt laughed. "I'm sure you will. Tell the crew hello, about the lovely early evening I'm having, and that I'm not at all rubbing it in."

Elaine waved but since she was already in discussion with Rick, she didn't pay them more attention.

"I for one am so ready to be done. Thank goodness we're done. We're done, aren't we?" Wiley didn't mean to whine, but he might be whining just a bit. "Did we know tomorrow had no filming?"

"It's on the call sheet I am going to tell you about. Elaine beat me to the punch." Holt absently massaged Wiley's neck.

Wiley tried not to tense up from how good it felt.

"It is good to be done." Holt exhaled. "I keep wondering if I'll get pangs or realize I'll miss this, but I don't think I'm going to miss this."

"Is that weird? Also, it's okay if it's weird. It's also *also* okay to not miss it."

Holt turned toward Wiley. "I appreciate that."

He seemed to get briefly lost in thought and then opened his mouth to say more. Kit interrupted, trilling a loud yoo-hoo while trotting over to meet them at the car.

"That was good today. You're doing really great, Wiley. I knew you'd take it seriously, but this is better than I'd hoped." Kit sounded actually sincere. "We're doing this! It's working and we're making it work and we're gonna pull it off. Enjoy your lovely early evening, Holty."

"I will. At least until rehearsal."

"Oh, that's right. The dance!" Kit struck a dance frame and sauntered sideways while humming a tango. "My gift to you." He kept dancing from them when Elaine called, "Don't forget Glen and Janet. Toodles!"

"Glen?" Wiley asked. "And Janet the very efficient PA?"

Holt sighed and looked toward the people hurrying their way.

"Glen. Extra cameraman and fill-in-wherever guy. Janet here to help him, I'm sure." Holt pursed his lips as they neared. "Hiya, what's up? Elaine said we're all finished and it's way before nine, but even so, I didn't think the rehearsals were being filmed."

"They're not? I mean, no, I'm not and they're not. We're going with you to pick out village houses." Glen patted his bag, bulging with gear. "Wherever that is and whatever they're for. Ready?"

HOLT held in an exasperated sigh as Wiley nervously tidied his very tidy house while Glen and Janet got set up.

Wiley's nerves got under his skin. This wasn't a big deal and no reason to be nervous or rearrange the couch pillows, but he didn't intervene in case Wiley took it wrong, and it wasn't fair to say "hey, calm down, unexpected filming in your house when you really wanted to be finished for the day is no biggie." He also just didn't like that Wiley was out of sorts.

Glen and Janet weren't at fault. It wasn't even that bad—they were going to livestream for a half hour and then they'd pack up and go.

But Holt had been looking forward to a break from performing. From the camera and everyone who thought he and Wiley were eagerly anticipating getting married in a few short weeks. He also looked forward to seeing the house again and having the chance to check out projects and repairs he remembered doing.

Some downtime to discuss filming so far, work on their stories, and agree about how to proceed would have been helpful too.

When Wiley refolded the quilt over the back of the couch and started in with the pillows again, Holt stepped from his out-of-the-way spot by the front door to get into Wiley's path and between him and Glen's view.

"Hey. You gonna be okay?"

Wiley chuckled weakly. "Sure, I'm fine. This is fine. It's what I agreed to after all, so." He shrugged.

"Hm." Holt pried a pillow from Wiley's two-handed grip and let it drop onto the couch. "At least we have a task we can focus on. We're raiding a village—could be fun. We can set to it with long matches and cocktail forks."

Wiley's reluctant smile made Holt's heart lift.

"I made certain with Kit that the majority of our dance lesson wouldn't be filmed. He agreed it might be too complicated, but the trade-off is I'll post selfies and short videos to the show's social." Without thinking about it, Holt loosely circled Wiley's wrists with his hands and massaged them, working up to relax Wiley's clenched fists. Wiley sighed but relaxed, and that made him smile. "We get through this, and then we have all day tomorrow. Think you can make it?"

"I can. If…."

"If?"

"You let go of me so I can redo the pillows one last time."

"I guess. If you insist and must."

"I definitely must." Wiley tugged to get free.

Holt briefly tightened his hold, and on an instinct that felt right as anything, brought Wiley's knuckles to his lips for a light kiss. Wiley pulled away, fists clenched again.

"Okay, well. Okay." Holt start-stopped but then moved aside and returned to the mat by the front door.

Wiley redid the pillows and darted into the kitchen. Janet changed the pillows so none remained in the center of the couch and cleared off the coffee table.

"You guys sit here, and we'll film from there." She pointed at the deep bay windowsill the couch faced. "It'll be more homey and intimate than the kitchen table or standing around."

Holt didn't linger on wanting to linger on *homey and intimate*.

"What?"

"What what?" Holt popped an eyebrow at Janet.

"You're smiling in a certain kinda secretive way. So, what are you thinking?" Janet spread her hands. "It could give us a better shot or narrative insight."

"You definitely picked that up from Kit." Holt cast about for a reason to be smiling in a certain kinda secretive way and hit on what wasn't a lie, exactly. "I remembered how Wiley's grandma made me sit on the windowsill instead of her furniture. Because I was dirty and sweaty from work and she said it'd break like twigs under me." He gestured around the room. "We could flip the shot. Wiley and I on the windowsill, you film from the couch. The azaleas are in bloom, which would be a good backdrop."

"Nice. I like it. And that's a great story—you should repeat it as we're filming." Janet called, "Wiley? You good?"

Wiley stared at Holt from the kitchen doorway. After a moment he said, "Does anyone need a drink? A snack?"

Holt considered suggesting they crack open a bottle of wine. Or whiskey.

"Thanks, no, we're good." Janet glanced at Glen. "Right?"

"Totally good." Glen gave the ubiquitous thumbs-up. "I'm ready to start filming. What do we think for this? It's going to be continuous, so let's get the blocking figured out."

Janet consulted her phone. "Something straightforward. Get the village down, put the houses on the table, go through them and make yes, no, and maybe piles."

"How about just yes and no?" Wiley asked.

"Everything is better in threes. Also, we don't want to give away your final choices yet. Leave that as a fun surprise on your wedding day." Janet slid past Holt to a closet. "You said there's a stepladder in here?"

"There is. Burrow past the coats to the back," Holt answered automatically. There always had been. He'd used it all the time when helping GB.

"Aha, yes. Thanks." Janet unfolded it and handed it to Holt. "We can start with this shelf," she said, gesturing to a frame directly under one shelf. Then she took a huge sidestep to stand under the other shelf. "You move to this one, and Glen will position in the kitchen to stay behind you as you move along and then to the windowsill. I'll get the houses to the coffee table off camera."

"Works for me. Wiley?" Holt held the ladder as Glen and Janet squeezed past into the kitchen.

"We don't have to pretend you're not here, right? Since this is the low-key streaming extras?" Wiley carefully placed the stepladder for best access to the first shelf.

"Right. Overall, don't pay much attention to the camera or worry about engaging with me or Glen, but show things to viewers and stuff if you want. It's not like show footage where the camera doesn't exist." Janet looked at them. "We good?"

"Start here, next shelf, maneuver to the windowsill, three piles of houses. Got it." Wiley nodded decisively. "Good."

"Great. I'm going to just hit Send here on the posts we have ready to go saying we're going live…." Janet's thumbs flew over her phone. "Okay! Let's do this." She slipped aside, tapped Glen on the shoulder, and held a finger to her lips.

Glen checked on them and then motioned that he'd started filming.

Holt grinned at the camera and allowed years of practice to take over. "Hi, everybody. If you read Kit's posts about what's going on for this episode, you'll know we're at Wiley's house to pick out centerpieces for our wedding reception tables. If you don't read Kit's posts about what's going on for this episode, first, don't tell him. Second, hey, guess what? We're at

Wiley's house to pick out centerpieces for our wedding reception tables."

"We're here to raid my grandma's village." Wiley's smile was adorable and a bit shy, but he didn't hide from the camera. He stepped into the gap between the stepladder and the wall and grabbed on to its curved back. "I'm going to stay down here, and Holt's doing all the dashing action stuff."

Holt easily followed the cue. "Well then, up I go. You know you don't have to hold a stepladder." He chuckled as Wiley stood fast. "Sure, all right." He climbed to the top step and started to hand the village pieces to Wiley one at a time, who passed them to a discreet Janet.

Holt was surprised at how sharp his memory was of installing these shelves and placing the village just so, according to GB's direction. There were several houses he didn't remember—he realized with a start how many years he hadn't been here or gotten to know Wiley better or kept track of them after he'd left for college—and at some point Wiley had added strings of solar LED lights to cast a gentle glow among the houses.

They moved on to the other shelf and repeated the process, Wiley stubbornly holding the stepladder steady and Holt retrieving the pieces.

"Last one." It was a red-and-white-striped lighthouse. "I always liked this one."

"Me too. Last one down, first one decided?" Wiley took the lighthouse and held it to his chest.

Holt nodded and climbed down, feeling like he towered over Wiley even back on the floor. It was a feeling he didn't mind. The shelves were generally clean, but a large piece of fuzz had dislodged from somewhere and landed in Wiley's hair. He huffed a breath at it, but it didn't budge.

"Just a sec." Holt wrapped a hand around the stepladder back and leaned in. He reached for the fuzz but didn't grab or flick it away. Wiley's upturned gaze and blush and quickened pulse distracted him wholly.

He traced Wiley's eyebrow with his outstretched finger and smiled at how silky it was. As silky as he'd imagined since recognizing Wiley in the park and stopping to say hello.

Wiley's cheek was hot under his touch and that made *his* pulse jump.

Compulsion led him to trace his finger from mole to mole on Wiley's face. He watched fine movements under Wiley's skin, nerves and muscle reacting to him. To his touch.

"You have a...." Holt lost his train of thought as Wiley followed his hand to press a cheek into his palm.

"Yes?"

Holt licked his lips and watched Wiley do the same. "This," he breathed, and kissed the rise of Wiley's brow, the heat in Wiley's cheek, and then the corner of Wiley's mouth.

He hovered over Wiley's lips. Not from uncertainty. From wanting Wiley to want his kiss.

Wiley hummed and tilted upward, shifting against his hand and pushing their mouths together. Holt grinned and let his other hand cup Wiley's ribs, and satisfaction thundered in him at the wild flutter of Wiley's heartbeat and breath. He came forward until his shins knocked into the stepladder. He barely noticed the painful sting because his full attention was on the feel and taste of Wiley's mouth opening for him.

There was no hesitancy or nerves now. Wiley had a handful of his shirt and kissed him measure for measure, tongue rasping along his and darting to trace his teeth and the bow of his lips. Holt groaned and moved so he could hook Wiley's waist with his arm, timed with an unconscious roll of his hips.

"Ahem." Janet's cough was quiet but shattering to Holt.

He pulled away abruptly and caught what would seem like a bizarre apology to Wiley just in time.

Wiley stared at him, one hand white-knuckling the lighthouse, the other flattened against Holt's chest.

Whether in denial or invitation, Holt couldn't tell. He wasn't sure he wanted to know.

Glen grinned at him as Holt lowered to sit on the windowsill. It appeared he'd stopped filming the kiss not long into it, as he was busy at the coffee table assembly of buildings and houses, focusing in on this or that.

"Thanks," Holt mouthed.

Glen would think he appreciated the privacy. Good enough.

He pulled in a deep breath and opened one arm in wide invitation.

To his profound relief, Wiley came and sat next to him. Not quite to tuck into his arm, but not in any way that would look like Wiley was avoiding doing so. Holt leaned forward, scooted the table toward them, and tried to stop the ringing in his head and the buzzing in his lips and chest and groin.

"How do we want to do this?"

Wiley moved the figurines to cram together at one end of the table. "Yes at the far end, maybe in the middle, and we can leave the nos here." He handed Holt the lighthouse. "Yes?"

Holt nodded, showed the lighthouse to the camera, and set it at the far end.

Wiley grabbed a quaint stone church, and they both said, "Yeah, no," simultaneously.

Holt laughed and watched humor blossom back into Wiley's eyes and relax around Wiley's mouth. Awkwardness from the kiss and stress and gladness all mixed together in a certain giddiness and made him laugh harder. Wiley curled forward into near giggles, and Holt's laughter turned softer, fond.

"I mean.... It's fine but... not quite for this occasion." Wiley caught his breath and put the church back down. They dismissed a vintage gas station and an ornate Victorian house just as quickly. He reached for a rustic barn but paused. "Okay, between yes and maybe—we need to have enough to choose from for the final settings, so we can't be too picky."

"Good point. So, yes to the barn for sure." He held it a moment and reflexively squeezed Wiley to him, remembering that alternative venue and their goat friends. "Look at this beaut," he said to the camera while turning the barn this way and that. "Two outright yeses. We're doing good." Holt reached across and worked the bakery and a gazebo from a cluster of buildings. "Maybe on these two?"

"Yes gazebo, maybe bakery." Wiley blushed again, staring at the gazebo.

Holt quickly looked away and distracted them by piling haystacks and fencing and an old truck at the no end. He lifted a stout tree with a treehouse built into it from the group and smiled.

"I thought I didn't want any from after I left for college, but this one has to be yes."

"Why would that make a difference?"

"I'm not sure, exactly. Call it odd sentimentality." Holt couldn't explain better. He also hadn't realized he felt that way until just now.

"That'll work." Wiley bumped into him. "But that could be an early acquisition—how do you know when I got that?"

"I don't remember moving it or dusting it or putting it on those shelves." Holt set the treehouse firmly in the yes pile. "And I would. Like the lighthouse and bakery and B and B."

Wiley bumped him again but kept pressed close this time.

"You're staying at the Fernleaf B and B in town, aren't you?"

Holt nodded.

"Then let's make it a maybe." Wiley put the white B and B with the red shutters and built-on porch on the flat of his palm and gave the camera a few steady minutes to focus on it.

Holt searched out the only other item he wanted as yes for sure. "Maybe this could be at our table." He cradled a house that closely resembled Wiley's, down to the cedar siding and large square-pane windows, in his hands.

"That was one of the first Grandma got. I think it started this whole thing." Wiley gestured at the scatter of sorted figurines. "I'm agreed—definite yes."

"And at our table?"

Wiley took the house and set it down. "We'll see."

Holt recognized it was ridiculous to mind Wiley being evasive, and evasion with good reason. He still minded.

"Good enough."

They worked through the remaining dozen-some figurines. The yes pile stayed smallest, while maybe and no were about equal.

"So that's maybe on the firehouse and park, no for the beach cottage and wishing well, yes on the little cabin." Holt scanned the table. "Anything else?"

Wiley looked at Holt, smiled, and slid the hardware store from maybe to yes. "I think with that, we're done."

"You heard the man." Holt shifted to get his arm around Wiley again and grinned at the camera. "I hope everyone who tuned in had fun watching us bicker over house hunting. What did you think? Tell us in the comments and talk to us on our various social platforms."

"I think you should tell Holt the treehouse isn't a yes." Wiley grinned cheekily and waved, then sat forward to move the pieces around.

Holt made a noise of mock outrage and then pretended similar busywork. They pushed the houses and figures without doing anything until Janet told them they'd stopped filming.

"Yup, done and done," Glen confirmed.

Wiley immediately stood and moved away from Holt.

"Great! That was great, you guys." Janet stood from the sofa and typed on her phone as she talked. "Oh good, we're already getting engagement—these livestreams are really popular. Can we help put anything away before we scram?"

"Thanks, but no. It's just a table and a few houses."
Wiley dug in a drawer and pulled out a notebook and
pen. "Do you want some coffee or anything?"

"Ugh, you're so nice. You're the best." Janet
shook her head at Glen, who had stepped closer with
an eager grin. "But we have to go and get the digitals to
production. Review the footage, add in the detail shots,
and grab some gauzy-lit smiley moments between the
two of you to the ongoing promo reels, that kind of
thing."

"Right. Okay, well. Thanks for coming over."
Wiley rolled his eyes and shook his head. He opened
the front door for them. "Have a productive night. See
you soon."

"Thank you for letting us barge in and all around.
That was actually fun—you two just pop with chemistry.
I mean, whew!" Janet fanned her face. "Wiley's starting
to gain a bit of a following—you should check it out.
But Holt, don't get jealous." She shot a finger pistol at
Holt. "Enjoy your day off tomorrow. A day not doing
work or fixing something or being on set. However will
you cope?"

"I'll think of something."

"Sleep," Wiley said, overlapping Holt. He flushed
and cleared his throat when Glen and Janet chuckled.
"No, I'm serious. Just sleep and a lot of it. I don't care
what anyone else does."

Janet shut her eyes and leaned back. "That sounds
amazing. Order in too—you can order in here, right?—
whatever. You've earned the little break."

"See ya, guys." Glen shuffled his equipment and
followed Janet down the short path to the curb.

Wiley watched them drive away and stayed
standing, looking out the door.

"Janet made a good point. What should we do tomorrow?"

"I hadn't really thought about it. Aside the sleeping thing, which I was serious about. Carla might need help at the bakery. And I have some stuff around the house I should do." Wiley shrugged and finally closed the door. "What are you going to do?"

Holt hadn't considered they'd do anything separate. He hadn't envisioned a big day of plans for them exactly, but he had taken it for granted they'd do whatever might happen together. He skipped over sleep—six hours max was a lot for him, and also it was too easy here in Wiley's house, surrounded by memories, to imagine Wiley warm and pliant and soft in bed—and came up with "I'll help. You. At the bakery or around here." He added carelessly, "If you want."

Wiley didn't answer immediately. He went to the kitchen and rustled around, and Holt hated the uncertainty that crept into him as the silence stretched.

He studied the houses and figures and checked his phone. Several messages from Kit, reminding him of this and that and mentioning how cute the village selection went, some notes from Elaine, and a picture from Rick he opened without thinking about it.

Thought you'd like this one read Rick's message.

Holt did, a lot, and he wasn't sure what to make of that.

Rick had caught him and Wiley unguarded at lunch today, Wiley's coffee mug held in both their hands, the two of them leaned into each other laughing.

Holt closed the photo and moved on to his social accounts, where a heated debate on the pros and cons of the treehouse was already being hashed out. This whole brother-of-the-star-of-the-show and livestream angles were playing well and might just work. Might just give them each what they'd bargained for.

He looked up to Wiley standing in the kitchen doorway and wondered for a moment if it was what he still wanted.

Wiley carried two glasses of lemonade in. He gave one to Holt and sat on the sofa with the notebook and pen.

"That would be fine. Nice. Fine." Wiley twiddled the pen. "Let's make our yes-but-never-happening choices, you can take pictures for the florist or whatever, I'll talk Carla into feeding us dinner, and then we can go to the dance lesson."

"Oh God, that." Holt groaned. "How do I always manage to convince myself I've forgotten we're learning a dance?"

"I LOVE breakfast for dinner. Also, I can't believe it was only this morning we were here—feels like a year." Wiley had another bite of the egg, bacon, and cheese croissant Carla had thrown together for them. "Anyone who disagrees is a fool."

"Feels like two years at least. And hooray breakfast at any hour. Good thing I'm no fool." Holt popped the last bite of one sandwich into his mouth and grabbed another. "Well. About most things."

Carla thoughtfully ate a piece of bacon and leaned her elbows on the counter. "Great, so you both like breakfast food. But it's not so easy as me making a breakfast-themed cake—which I won't be doing, for the record. If you get my drift."

"Uh, so, no stack of pancakes artfully sculpted from fondant?" Wiley drew a blank. "Not that I'd want that but, no. I don't get your drift. Do you?"

Holt munched his sandwich and covered his mouth to say, "Not really, except being prepared is always half the battle."

Carla rolled her eyes. "You two are the worst. How can you run a total con job without knowing the scheme? Your favorite flowers? Don't just think you can wing it." She huffed. "You're past the big-ticket items Kit has more say on, so you're gonna have to start answering more granular questions about each other."

"How do you know?" Wiley sipped coffee as wariness crept up his spine.

"Because I watch the show, dingus. I've studied!" Carla harrumphed at them, went marching into the kitchen, and returned with a notebook covered in sticky tabs and scribbles. She slapped it down and opened it to a spread of densely filled pages. "Holt is usually not part of these segments because he's busy making the venue exactly right and building centerpieces and backdrops and whatnot. So while he's probably aware they happen, I'm guessing—since you guys looked like deer in the headlights hearing this from me, you should probably do more than *we like roses because roses are romantic*—that we gotta give these things the proper attention given our delicate situation."

"Whoa. That's some conspiracy theory level journaling. Do you have a corkboard and red string thing going in the kitchen? Holt knows the show, and Kit knows the score, so we're fine." Wiley glanced at Holt and didn't like the stillness of Holt's posture. "Aren't we?" The delicious sandwich suddenly felt leaden in his gut.

Wiley spun the notebook and scanned Carla's bullet lists and asides. It was quite thorough.

"We are. Mostly." Holt wiped his hands on a napkin and tugged the notebook over so they could both see it. "But Carla raises some fair points."

"This is more than fair points. This is serious business." Carla flipped to a different page. "We have to decide this stuff so you're ready. What are each other's favorite colors? Your perfectly personalized tokens of affection to swap during the reception? What flowers symbolize your love story? Kit will ask, and these are not things you want to be caught stammering lukewarm patch jobs when answering."

"Lukewarm patch jobs have been… sufficient so far," Wiley said almost confidently.

"Yes, because nothing says you're gonna pull this off like tepidly sufficient. That might work for random couple number sixteen in a season, but I don't know if you've noticed, and I'm guessing you haven't, your story has garnered a hella invested audience who are burning up comment sections and running rampant with speculation in the blogs about you two."

Cold nerves bolted through Wiley. "What kind of speculation? Like—they know we're total fakes speculation? Like I'm doing a horrible job and everyone's ironically amused? Like it's already over and we don't have to pretend anymore?"

The idea should elate him. It didn't.

Holt's hand covered his, sure and warm and gentle. He looked down to where he'd unwittingly started crumpling a corner of Carla's tin-hat notebook into his fist.

"Sorry about that." Wiley nudged the notebook back toward Carla. With his free hand.

"No. Quite the opposite. Which is why it's so dangerous."

"Yeah, that makes me feel 100 percent not better."

"Then I'm doing my job. This ratings boost Kit hoped for is going gangbusters." Carla waved expansively. "I can see it. There's appeal in the whole scenario. Huge hunky Holt, famous but reserved and notoriously private and always glad to be in the background, his adorbs little hometown boyfriend always so polite but funny, the grandma connection to swoon over, the cow eyes you make at each other like getting a glimpse at the *real* Holt and all because of Wiley, a romance kept secret until Kit lobbied the producers to let him plan the wedding of your dreams. It's heady stuff."

"You realize we're right here. And that it's fake."

Carla stuck her tongue out at Wiley. "So long as you realize what I'm reading online and vibing from the building buzz will come to bear, so you best be ready." She ripped pages from the back of the notebook. "I made a comprehensive list. You two should study it and figure out your answers—before you're on camera. Including how you're going to end it."

Holt sat forward. "How so?"

"I just think you'll need more than cold feet or whatever. Think of a compound reason, something with stakes attached. Viewers are invested, so not getting married will feel like a betrayal unless you get it right. I mean, you are leaving the show, so it might not matter overall. But, well. What a bummer for the show to go out on."

"Good to know." Holt's hand tightened over Wiley's. He took the list from Carla with his free hand. "So is this. I don't know why I didn't think of it first." His brow furrowed.

Carla's gaze bounced between them. Her eyebrows did some expressive things, but she didn't say more.

"We can work all this out tomorrow," Wiley suggested. "It shouldn't take long."

"Sure," Holt agreed absently and let Carla's list go. "I'm going to check in with Elaine, and then we can go?"

Wiley nodded and totally didn't shiver happily when Holt squeezed his hand and patted it twice before standing. Wiley had to hop from the tall stool—Holt just planted a foot and walked away. Holt peeked back at him, waved, and stepped outside, already tapping on his phone.

He looked back at Carla and felt a rising blush he couldn't suppress. "What?"

"What? I didn't say anything." Carla smiled, all butter-wouldn't-melt. She pressed her palms on the notebook. "Okay, I am smug about this and my smuggery is earned and legit. Thank goodness for me. You two would have been out at sea once Kit started asking you more personal questions. Why didn't this occur to either of you?"

"Details, details. We're managing. We'd have managed." Wiley's deflection didn't blunt Carla's sharp eyebrow raise. He just knew being with Holt had seemed natural and easy from the start and so he hadn't worried about the rest. Which was rational enough.

"Sure." Carla closed the notebook and reached into the bakery case for some brownies. "So, what's tomorrow? And where are you going next?"

"Tomorrow we have the day off filming. And a dance lesson." Wiley frowned. "Our intimacy assignment, a thing you and your book there should know all about."

"That we do! I think it was a bit over-the-top of Kit when it could have been like, grooms' table center doily macramé, but I have watched clips from your first lesson. You guys are super gonna have to cram for this final." Her grin faded as Wiley picked at a brownie without eating it. "Hey. You okay?"

"I'm fine," Wiley lied. He broke off a hunk of brownie and ate it as proof. "I just lose sight of how big all this actually is and then I really start thinking about it and it's a lot."

"I didn't mean to overwhelm you with my notebook of doom."

"No, I appreciate it. It's good. I'd way rather be overwhelmed over breakfast-for-dinner sandwiches in an empty bakery with brownies to soothe me than on camera."

"Whew, good. But for real, put your heads together and figure this out." Carla pushed her list at Wiley with purpose.

Wiley tried not to panic as he scanned her pages of notes and the list of things to consider. He'd have to have known Holt his entire life to answer. Not this whatever they were doing instead.

"Wiley? Overwhelmed looks like it's about to do a hostile takeover here."

He breathed in deeply and exhaled slowly.

Carla gripped Wiley's shoulders. "I got you. We can do this."

Wiley made a determined face. "We so can. We are."

"Yes." She thumped his arms and then fell back onto her heels. "You still seem a little freaked, though."

He was. Because he realized he wanted to know Holt's favorite color and scent and scented candle, and candles or twinkling lights for a centerpiece. He even had some inklings and was desperate to discover if his instincts were correct.

That and thinking about spending the entire day with Holt tomorrow, only the two of them working out their cover story—lies but very personal truths—was suddenly too intense.

"Can we come help you tomorrow? For part of the day at least? I don't know what we have planned other than this now, thanks to you, but all day doing this is too much."

The bell on the front door tinkled, and Carla looked past Wiley. "So, tea to go?" she called to Holt.

"That would be amazing." Holt pocketed his phone as he crossed to the counter. He leaned in to grab a brownie and stayed casually pressed along Wiley's side. "All quiet on the front."

"Okay. Good." Wiley didn't know what Holt might report otherwise and what that would require of them.

"I made them both how Wiley prefers. Milk, no sugar." Carla handed one to Holt. "He can have yours if that's not to your liking."

Holt had a sip and his low moan kinda sorta curled Wiley's toes.

"No, that's perfect."

"Hah, nice. Something in common you didn't have to preplan. And you can have more tomorrow morning, as much as you want. Since you have the day off, I'm nabbing you to help—we've had a run on everything since your episode started filming, and I could use some extra hands for a few hours." Carla handed Wiley the other to-go cup and winked. "Come around five."

"I think we can manage that. Yeah?" Wiley turned to Holt.

"Yeah. So long as I'm not expected to make anything. I'm a terrible cook."

Carla nodded solemnly and walked them to the front door. "Oh, there'll be plenty. Now, have fun dancing and then get some rest. See you bright and early."

"Sounds ominous, but can do. Thanks for dinner and brownies and this." Holt raised his cup.

Wiley kissed her cheek on the way out and whispered, "Thank you."

She gave him a fierce look. "Stay focused. You can do this." Then she pushed him out and locked the door.

"Have you given any thought about the trip you want to take? Production can book whenever—we won't make you wait three months to save a little on airfare."

"I have not. I probably should, but other things have managed to dominate my attention."

"Imagine that," Holt teased. He glanced around. "Maybe somewhere tropical. Or a history-rich city in Europe. Or a boat tour of Japan. Plenty of options."

Wiley bit back the impulse to ask where Holt would go. This was his trip to take, his reward. Holt already had plans to go—away from the show.

As they walked the few blocks to the studio, Wiley took in the groupings of benches, baskets of flowers hanging from the lampposts, the cozy glow of the storefronts Odalia had fought to rejuvenate. Cinnamon hung in the air from whatever Carla was baking, mingling with smoke and spices from the Indian restaurant on the corner. Their feet scraped pleasantly on the damp aggregate sidewalk, and the courthouse clock at the end of the block showed almost nine, as behind them church bells rang out the time, low and mellow.

It was nice. Contentedly nice. Familiar but not humdrum.

Wiley had noticed all those elements before, of course. But he'd never thought about them while walking next to Holt with reminders he'd wanted to flee, and wondering where that needful escape should lead after Holt was gone from his life, chasing around in his head.

They climbed the stairs to the studio to find Sarah, light-footed and elegant, sweeping around the room to their song.

"We should just let her dance for us," Holt murmured as they set down their things and went to stand where she gestured them. "Hello, Miss Sarah."

"Gentlemen, good evening. Since it's late I'd like to work for only an hour on some fundamentals. Yesterday was instructive for me about your instincts and movement dynamics." Sarah positioned them with a firm, efficient touch. "I'm no essentialist, so this has nothing to do with the height difference, but it's clear Holt should lead. Wiley, you make a perfect follow. If you would, take hold of each other in a dance frame that feels natural."

She pushed at their shoulders and spines and adjusted their stance.

"And Wiley, don't take that as a backhanded compliment—leading is easy. A perfect follow? Few and far between." Her tone was as crisp as her command of them and the boards. She started the song again and sent Holt into motion with a grip on his upper arm. "Get the sense of this in your bodies. The posture, the lift in your carriage, staying balanced on the balls of your feet. Good."

Wiley wasn't sure what dance they hobbled through. She told them to step, quick quick, slow slow, quick quick, slow slow. It wasn't a waltz and obviously no tango, but he didn't know the difference from there.

"Tell me, Miss Sarah, what are we learning?" Holt watched their feet as they crossed the floor.

"Ah, up here, please." Sarah tipped Holt's chin so he looked up again. "This is a simple sway step. More or less a twostep and quite slow to match your music. After you get the step, we'll add some flourishes and turns."

Wiley grimaced.

"At the corners of your dance space, dearest. I had Kit measure the reception area and marked that off here so you learn within safe boundaries." Laughter played around Sarah's mouth. "I'm not going to make Holt spin you about or attempt any lifts. My aim is to have you perform with effortless confidence, more than anything else. So together we'll learn a dance that doesn't outmatch your skills in the time we have to master it."

"Thank goodness for that. Anything more and I would for sure launch him into the woods or something." Holt's hold on Wiley tightened.

"It's what any skilled dance teacher should do— for her students and herself. Now, stay loose, please. There we go." Sarah continued to call in cadence for them to step, quick quick, slow slow.

They repeated that from one end of the studio to the other until Sarah's voice became a meaningless drone and Wiley's movements automatic.

"Yes! That's it. You're both doing better than I could have hoped." Sarah brought them to a halt and left them to stand at a curved strip of tape on the floor.

"Let's try a direction change. Holt, bring Wiley here and let this guide you to your left."

Holt looked down and lifted a foot.

"Up please, thank you. There you are. Keep going."

Holt huffed in his throat and looked up.

Wiley couldn't keep from smiling.

"Shush, perfect follow." Holt set his shoulders and traveled toward Sarah.

Wiley snickered when Holt's gaze fell to watch the ground as they passed the curving tape.

They got stuck at the far end, not quite managing to clear their feet and the twist of their hips to continue smoothly around the room. But it wasn't completely horrible. Three steps from the line and they stalled out.

"That simply gives us something to work on." Sarah clapped twice and returned to their side. "Overall, a promising start."

"How carefully positive, thank you." Holt grinned wryly.

Midway through another loop of their song, Sarah's phone chimed. "Ah, my alarm." She retrieved it from the sound system on the back wall of shelves, her flowy layers billowing like a regal cloud as she moved.

"Yeah, you're right," Wiley whispered.

"Hm? About what?"

"She should just dance for us instead."

"I don't know." Holt shifted his hold from Wiley's hip to the small of Wiley's back. "She said we have a promising start. Things to work on. That seems worth pursuing."

Wiley went still, and his gaze locked with Holt's.

Holt curled their hands to his chest and kept Wiley close, watching Wiley as he led them through several quick quick, slow slow steps.

Billie's end notes drifted to silence, and they drifted to a stop.

"Perhaps I should rethink my choreography." Sarah laughed. "Class is over. Thank you, gentlemen, for your hard work. I'd like for you to practice tomorrow and then see you again at nine. We'll deal with those turns."

"Yes, ma'am," Wiley answered automatically.

Holt let go and stepped back. A quick chill chased over Wiley—Holt put out heat like a furnace.

"Would you indulge us with some selfies and get a short video of us dancing?" Holt got his phone out. "I promised Kit I'd document some teasers."

"Certainly." Sarah patted her hair and struck a pose between them.

Holt snapped several pictures and turned the phone over to Sarah to get some of them in their dance frame. She set the music back up and then began a soft count. Holt nodded, mouthing along as he got the rhythm, and managed several steps for her to record. Wiley was awkward, too aware of the camera, and he couldn't ignore the nagging burden and worries of his agreement, the show, learning a dance to never perform.

"Relax, Coy." Holt smiled and spun them. "You're perfect, remember."

Wiley had to brace a hand on Holt's shoulder, but it did make him laugh as Holt spun them once more.

"All right, I've turned it off." Sarah brought Holt's phone over. "You're free to go. Remember your homework, including what I always say, getting some rest."

"Yes, of course, Miss Sarah. Thank you again for your time." Holt held his arm out to Wiley. "Shall we?"

Wiley scoffed but took it. Not for long. The doorway and stairs were too narrow for them to both fit.

Holt took possession of his arm once they were back outside. "Can I walk you home?"

"How gallant. Ballroom clearly does something for you. Even if you aren't perfect like me quite yet."

"How ungallant." Holt hummed their song as they walked along. Subtle laughter threaded his deep, off-key notes.

At the corner, Wiley stopped. "The Fernleaf and my house are in opposite directions from here. And in too few hours, Carla will be bossing us around."

"You state a compelling case." Holt turned in and slid his hands to hold Wiley's wrists. "Then it's good night."

Wiley couldn't deny Carla's earlier assessment of Holt being handsome, a total hunk. The gossamer lamplight showcasing his strong profile and glow from the spring fog only enhanced that.

Holt came forward and seemed about to do or say something, but after a beat he started walking backward. He wagged a finger. "Get some rest."

"Since I'm about to pass out, I'll have little say in the matter."

"Hah, same. See you tomorrow." Holt turned to skip lightly over the curb and dart across the street.

Wiley stood watching until he disappeared.

His walk home was short and lonely, and for the second night, he went through the motions of quick chores, mail, shower, and fell exhausted into bed.

But not exhausted enough to avoid staring at the ceiling, thinking far too much about Holt.

Chapter Four

FIVE arrived, too early and unwanted, but Wiley had given up on sleep and headed for the bakery at four thirty. He was bleary-eyed and yawning, so Carla shoved a vat of coffee into his hands, sat him in the comfy wingback chair in the corner of the kitchen, and told him to warm up a little so he didn't ruin anything.

"What else are you doing with your day?"

Wiley blinked into his coffee and shrugged. "Go for a long walk? Laundry? Put the village away? Wide-open possibilities here."

Carla planted a floury hand on her hip. "Did a village get misplaced?"

"Grandma's village—you know, it sits on the shelves over the windows at home. We're using houses as reception centerpieces. It's a whole—" He frowned at her smile. "You watched the stream. You know what I'm talking about. Stop testing me so early in the morning."

"That seems like a very not-Kit decision."

"It is because it wasn't." Wiley chuckled. "I unwittingly took the wrong cue and went with the wrong choice filming the décor segment. But—ask me if I mind dot com."

"Ooh, a bit of rebellion. I approve." Carla grabbed Wiley's apron from its peg and tossed it toward him. "You're talking in multisyllables and full sentences. Time to start the caramel cranapple scones."

"Yes, ma'am." Wiley stretched as he stood and downed the rest of his coffee. He wrapped into the apron and brought the ties around front, making a tight knot low at his waist.

A cool draft swept behind him as he soaped up and scrubbed his hands.

"I always feel so official and ready to tackle anything once I have this thing on. Totally dorky but totally true."

"You look official and ready to tackle anything. Do I get one?"

Wiley almost twisted his head off turning to see Holt standing in the open back door. He fought a spontaneous huge grin and also started yawning again, so he figured he wound up looking like an angry gargoyle.

"Good morning. Am I late?" Holt accepted the mug of coffee Carla handed him. "Manna from heaven, thank you."

"Have as much as you want—that and the tea I promised yesterday. And nope. Wiley's early, and five is well after I get started every day. No big."

"Glad to hear it. The endless caffeinated beverages part especially. I've never worked in a bakery, so I'd hate for my first day to be a disaster."

"Morning," Wiley said thickly after yawning again. He rummaged in a box of linens on one of the wire shelving racks and dug out an enormous blue-ticked apron. Some kitchen supply company had sent it as promotional swag after they'd opened, and he and Carla had laughed at its hugeness and took a picture with them both in it. It was decided the apron was faulty and sent to them to get rid of it as much to sell them on the company's silicone baking trays and trivets.

That picture was still on the friends-and-family wall that ran from the bakery's front door to the start of the glass cases. Which reminded him he hadn't updated the pictures in a while, and since Carla had started baking pet treats and the clientele included some very good dogs, he really should.

"Here, this might fit." Wiley tossed Holt the apron.

Holt caught it with one hand and slithered from his pullover with the other. The apron fit—snugly across the chest and not a lot of overlap from tying it at the front like Wiley had—and he looked stupidly attractive in his navy blue V-neck, the apron, and fawn cargo pants.

Wiley grumped, washed his hands again, and started assembling bowls and ingredients for the scones.

"Well." Holt thrust both arms out and spread his hands. "Put me to use."

The near-pornographic cascade of ideas and imagery that provoked in Wiley made him have to actually stop mid-egg-crack and catch his breath.

"How do you feel about hauling some huge sacks of flour and other ingredients around? I've outgrown the pantry but haven't done much about it."

Holt chuckled in anticipation. "Lead the way."

Wiley shuddered from the nape of his neck down. He did not turn from the counter to watch Holt heft and lift and reorganize, work they'd put off doing for months because everything was too cumbersome to deal with.

He'd finished the scones and had rolls going when Carla sidled up to Wiley.

"Bakery brawn, I'm swooning."

She refilled his coffee so he didn't accidentally douse her with nonstick spray.

"Scones and rolls already. You've been busy." Carla nudged Wiley. "Come on, come see how amazing it looks."

Wiley rubbed buttery flour from his hands and followed her to the pantry. It wasn't a separate room, more a clever arrangement of shelving units and bins that had depth and height for storage.

"See? He figured out how to join the top wire shelves with boards so there's even more space and stability. There's hooks—hooks!—he made from some of the old cooling racks we no longer use, for hook-hanging things, and he reconfigured the bins all to one side so we don't have to fight past them to get small stuff like spices." Carla gave Holt a squeezy hug. "This is so good."

Holt grinned. "I try."

Wiley could tell Holt's grin was genuine. Pleasure and satisfaction radiated from him.

The closest he'd seen to that since getting into all this was during their dance lessons when Holt didn't mash his foot or do a quick on the slow or a slow on the quick.

"What next?" Holt rubbed his hands together and threw a happy, sexy grin over his shoulder at Wiley as Carla led him into the front area.

Wiley admired the admittedly much improved pantry area and then kneaded his finished dough with a bit more force than usual.

As he worked he settled into the familiar tasks, reassured by the rote processes and known outcomes, and he smiled hearing Holt and Carla banter and bang things around. He wasn't a baker and never had aspirations for it, but doing this for Carla had never been in question. Of course he'd helped; of course he showed up for half wages and all the day-old goodies he could take; of course he did what he could to make it a success. Along the way he discovered he still didn't hold aspirations to be a baker, but he did like the work.

It was a creative outlet of sorts, let him use his hands without worrying about color choices or material pricing or centimeter details like when designing products.

The all-he-could-want day-old goodies part was pretty great too.

"Wiley, get in here," Carla called from the doorway.

He finished getting scones onto the cooling racks and slid rolls and Carla's croissants into the oven and went where she beckoned.

"Whoa." He halted stock-still, even absently wiping his hands on his apron.

The front of the building had a long bank of nearly floor-to-ceiling windows. He and Carla had talked about doing some interesting feature there but hadn't had the budget or the chance, so the line of bistro tables remained. He guessed the chance was the few hours he'd been absorbed in scones and rolls.

In place of the bistro tables was a raised platform that undulated along the windows, and on it were the love seat no one sat in that used to sit under the photo wall, and several crates turned into low tables and benches. It was casual and inviting but polished, and Wiley had no idea how they'd pulled it off.

"Right?" Carla gushed at his astonishment. "Look." She pointed out the window to where a production truck was parked and then pointed at Holt. "He called and over a couple dudes came—not quite as brawny but as handy. We even livestreamed it. I mean, who's up at this hour, but we figured why not. And we got those upholstered armless chairs from the weird room, see?"

He did. The weird room would one day be another bathroom, they hoped. The armless chairs were relics of the building's past, in vintage raised velvet prints that were appealing again. Some were at the dining tables in the seating area, and some were in groups under the photo wall with more crate-table things.

Stupid, awkward tears welled up, and Wiley coughed to hold them back. "It looks good. It looks so good." He smiled weakly. "I guess this means you can keep the apron."

"Oh-ho, now that's a deal." Holt crossed to him and led him onto the platform. He bounced and grinned and kept hold of Wiley's hands. "Super sturdy, no squeaks. We made it out of salvage pallets and lumber odds and ends from the set. I knew we had loads of MDF no one needed in one of the trucks."

"MDF?"

"This stuff." Holt tapped his toe on the wide hunks of smooth wood sheathing the existing floor. "Particle board meets plywood."

"I might paint it tonight after closing. I haven't decided." Carla hopped up and fell onto the sofa. "The raw state isn't bad, though. Rustic, goes with the exposed HVAC and pipes and mismatched tin ceiling."

"Your tin ceiling is incredible. I don't even want to price what it'd cost in today's market." Holt turned to Wiley, and his grin softened to an almost pensive expression. "Do you really like it?"

"What? Do I like it. I lo—" Wiley licked his lips and for some reason couldn't say the rest. "*This* is incredible. Honestly."

Holt's grin didn't return. Instead his eyes narrowed, burning with something Wiley didn't try to define.

"I can't believe you did all this."

"Not a big job to me and the boys." Holt shrugged. "I wasn't lying that I'm a crap cook, but this? This kind of stuff I can do."

"I'll say. Thank you."

"I hoped you'd like it. It's for you." Holt's hands tightened around Wiley's. "And Carla. The bakery."

Wiley went onto his toes and kissed Holt, short and sweet and square on the mouth. Holt caught him and held him fast and kissed him back. Enough to steal his breath and share a dart of heat and wetness from the seeking reach of their tongues. Then he rocked back when Holt pulled away, swung their arms in a few weird flaps, and let go to stride outside to the truck.

Carla raised an eloquent eyebrow from her perch on the love seat.

"Ehhh," Wiley grunted. "Don't." He ducked his head and went back into the kitchen to check the rolls.

"So. Uh." Carla rapped the doorframe and stared at him bug-eyed a few moments later. "We kind of are swamped? And by kind of I mean there's a line out the door, as apparently superfans are in town and one of them saw the livestream, but there's also curious people from town who know you and Holt are here and also the regulars? So. Gird your loins and good luck."

She nodded decisively, straightened her shoulders, and marched the trays of rolls to the display cases.

The next several hours were a blur.

But a good blur. A busy, tons of chatty customers free with their money and patient for their drinks and donuts and croissants blur. A no time to think about kissing Holt and Holt kissing him back and wanting to keep kissing Holt blur.

It amazed him how many people said they couldn't wait to meet him or wanted a quick hello or picture.

Wiley trotted miles, between slinging bacon and drinks and trips to the kitchen, ovens, racks, and bakery cases. He kept Holt in the corner of his eye, noting the broad smile plastered on Holt's face was the TV-grin he'd come to recognize, and not the pleased one from when it was just them and the pantry redo. That gave him a boost as he zoomed from the kitchen, loaded with rolls and cookies from dough Carla had the quick thinking to get from the freezer.

"Okay, everyone! Attention please. I'm sorry to say we're sold out," Carla yelled over the hubbub. "I'm glad to get anyone a drink or some water if you've been waiting, but every last crumb is gone."

Some groans and ineffectual shuffling not moving toward the door was the response.

"Hey, if you didn't get a cupcake or danish or whatever, let's get a selfie." Holt had been working nonstop in the seating area, delivering plates of goodies and refilling coffee and being generally stupidly charming. He sat on the platform in front of the love seat and thumped it. "C'mon, group hug time."

The disappointment lifted from the last waiting customers as they crowded around Holt, cramming on the love seat and tucking behind him and under his arm as he held the other one way out to get the shot.

"Anyone mind if I post this?" Holt asked as he checked the photo and started tapping the screen.

A resounding chorus of "No!" was his answer, and he laughed.

"Fantastic. Look for it on my social—tag yourself and comment if you're in the picture or are milling about not wanting in the picture but not wanting to leave yet."

Light laughter rose from the bakery as groups of fans and lookie-loos studied the picture wall and posed in the armless chairs or at the front door painted with Carla's logo.

Holt held the phone out again and showed the selfie around. "There, don't we look so good?"

The group of mostly women around him cooed and giggled and were definitely mollified.

"Can we get one with you in it?" a woman called to Wiley from the love seat. She was plump and cheerful in a red sweater and matching red eyeglasses and had her arms around two younger, much more fashionably dressed women. "My daughters and I love the show, and this episode has been amazing so far. You guys are so adorable."

"Me?" Wiley asked even as Carla had him push-marched around the display cases and over to Holt.

She gave a little shove and Holt took over, catching Wiley in the cradle of his chest and legs to sit on the platform, and keeping him there for another few selfies.

"I'm posting this one too, everyone," Holt said to their cheers. He kissed Wiley's temple. "Okay, up you get."

Wiley got practically dead-lifted to a stand, Holt rose behind him, and Wiley thought about the hard, strong, muscly thighs he'd just sat on and blanched, then blushed.

"Thank you." The woman who'd asked stepped from the platform and shook Wiley's hand. "This has been the best day already! Congratulations on the wedding. But really, the marriage—that's the important part."

"Too right," Holt smoothly cut in, dropping an arm around Wiley's waist as Wiley only stared. "And we thank all of you for showing up this morning, and your good wishes. Wow." He covered his heart with a hand. "I'm near tears, but that's because you got all the danishes before I had one. I won't hold it against you."

He laughed with the utterly charmed group and gently but firmly ushered them all toward the door, gathered the stragglers, and got everyone outside and the door locked behind them.

Carla slid her arm in front of them to lower the shade, and they stood for a bit in the sudden quiet.

"There's a few weirdly shaped danishes, two slightly overdone croissants, and one crushed cupcake in the back." Carla looked from Holt to Wiley. "Race you." She darted off.

"Unfair advantage," Holt called after her.

A sticky "Hah!" drifted to them from the kitchen.

Wiley exhaled. "So. I was a disaster."

"No." Holt's whole face wrinkled earnestly. "You kept up with the crush way better than me. I walked in circles pretending like I know how to wait tables."

"Not that part. The selfies and small talk with fans—why do I even have fans? I don't have fans—part. I'm not good at small talk, period. Small-talking strangers eager for a glimpse of you was a whole new level of not good at."

Holt scoffed. "You were fine. Not one of them left here thinking you are anything but as cute and polite and funny and kind as they hoped." He started toward the kitchen. "Come on before Carla eats everything. And don't worry overly about it either. Just like getting used to being on camera takes practice, so does being around fans. I wasn't good at small talk at first for sure."

"I'm sure you also did fine. You've always been polite and funny and kind too." Wiley chuckled and followed Holt behind the display cases and prep area. "I bet Kit had it down from moment one."

"But not cute?"

Wiley stopped. "What?"

"So you think I'm polite, funny, kind," Holt counted off on a hand. "But not cute?"

"Nope," Wiley said too quickly.

Holt looked aggrieved.

Wiley blushed and made big eyes. "You're not the cute type, is all."

"Hm—so what type am I?"

Holt swiveled toward Wiley. His tone hadn't changed much, but it was enough. Deepening, a resonance, not giving anything away, but Wiley got the definite sense Holt wanted to know his answer.

"Is cute bad?" Holt ran a light fingertip along Wiley's jawline. "I don't think it is."

"No. It's good. I don't mind—I mean. You know." Wiley shook his head. "You're very handsome, okay? I wasn't implying you're lacking in the looks when I said—didn't say—that."

"Very handsome is nice. I like very handsome." Holt wasn't teasing. He laid his thumb on Wiley's chin and closed his eyes before taking in a long breath, but after a moment he stepped back again. "Thank you."

Wiley's thoughts were too muddled to form an answer and his skin where Holt had touched him was on fire, which was an added distraction he didn't need.

"Get in here if you want anything! I'm about to devour the rest," Carla yelled in an effective interruption. "Croissant?" she asked Wiley as he walked into the kitchen after Holt.

He gratefully accepted it and the coffee she had ready and slumped into the comfy chair.

"That was incredible. I hope it never happens again." Carla laughed. "What a ravenous horde! And I'm not talking about the locust effect on the food. People bought all the T-shirts and buttons we had lying around from our grand opening, asked if they could have or buy the paper doilies from the display cases and the creamers and sugar bowls, I caught someone trying to sneak into the kitchen 'for a look around,' and at least three spoons are missing. It's a good thing I use mismatched sets of everything, found at thrift shops."

"Yikes, I'm so sorry." Holt dropped his danish and started doing a spot inspection.

"It is okay. Really." Carla pushed from her lean on the counter and pulled Holt back to the bench he'd been on. "I'm actually glad to have the T-shirts and buttons off my hands. Now I can justify making more to commemorate your episode happening—and sell them online."

"I'd say they mean well, which most do, but it is a lot. I had no idea that many fans were even in town. We've heard a few rumblings of minor thefts around town. I hope it's not related." Holt frowned. "At least let production reimburse you for the spoons. And if you find anything else missing."

Carla waved him off. "That doesn't seem necessary, especially after what you and the crew did for me this morning."

"I mean it. Firmly. That bit of lumber and time isn't a fair trade—this is." Holt got out his phone. "I'm texting Elaine right now that you'll get her an invoice including if you went over your planned budget on baking goods to keep up with the crush, starting today through end of filming. You might not get an apocalyptic swarm again, but they will be back."

"How ominous." She wrinkled her nose. "Pride would like me to refuse—but yes, it's a deal. Thank you." Carla rolled against the edge of the counter and stood hip-shot so she could write in the ideas notebook she always kept handy. "I'm reminding myself to get you an invoice. And designing that commemorative T-shirt tonight."

Wiley listened through a pleasant doze, but that got his attention. "I can do that for you."

"You have enough on your plate as it is. I might not even have as many plates to wash today as usual."

"Don't be silly. I still have the art and files from the grand opening design, and mine will look way better." Wiley finished his coffee and made himself stand. "It won't even take an hour."

"But this is your day off." Carla pouted, but her eyes danced in hopeful anticipation. "I don't want you to, but I really want you to."

"I know." Wiley kissed her cheek and dumped his dishes in the sink. "I'll let you clean up alone. Fair trade."

"Done."

"Okay, then I'm away. I will upload the design and make a product page for it and text you." Wiley walked comically slow toward the door and then paused once he had it open. "Okay. Have fun cleaning." He glanced at Holt but didn't want to make demands or have groundless expectations. "Yup, g'bye."

Carla crossed her arms and opened her mouth, but before she said whatever she looked ready to admonish, Holt jammed the rest of the danish in his mouth, downed his coffee, and took his dishes to the sink.

"Hold up, Coy—I'll come with you. Those village houses aren't going to shelve themselves." He patted Carla's arm as he went past. "I had a great time. I think Elaine already talked to you some about setting up the cake stuff—but let me know if you have any questions or if Kit is being too relentless about any whim or detail. Talk soon."

Wiley waved and pushed the door so it'd swing wide, but he didn't wait. He couldn't risk Holt getting a good look at his huge grin and what had to be a too-pleased expression.

It didn't take much for Holt's long-legged stride to catch him.

Holt hooked Wiley's waist and drew them together, and the sudden sideways movement made it feel only natural for Wiley to let his head rest on Holt's chest.

"One for the lurking fans," Holt said lowly and kissed Wiley's forehead. He tightened his hold and settled them into an unhurried pace.

"Yes, of course." That dimmed some of the immediate pleasure from Holt's seemingly spontaneous kiss and gathering of him to keep close, but Wiley didn't pout.

A pout might be caught on camera and posted online and nitpicked for days, after all.

He didn't see anyone lurking but that didn't mean anything. Wiley didn't actually want to cause ripples of gossip and negative speculation. Any more than it didn't matter the kiss wasn't real.

Holt didn't let go as they approached his house, and so they bumped their way up the narrow path to his porch and front door. Wiley dug his key from the pocket sealed to Holt's side and put it in Holt's waiting palm. He grunted as Holt went in sideways and pulled him in after.

"I'm practicing," Holt said and, still without letting go, carefully turned them to face each other in the small space of his entryway. He changed his hold to a loose version of their dance frame and hummed a few bars over some not-terrible steps. "We are supposed to practice. I'm not facing Miss Sarah without it. She'd know in a half second we were lying anyway."

"Less."

Holt snickered and spun them in a wobbly circle.

Wiley's pique evaporated in Holt's arms. He could tell himself someone might be camped down the street with a telephoto lens and getting this shot through his bay window or a small troupe of fans had followed them and were reeling with delight hiding in a nearby bush. He should. He didn't.

The spell broke when his elbow whacked into the wall and Holt mashed his foot.

"Good thing we're practicing," Wiley said dryly. The stinging vibrations running through him warbled in his voice.

Holt lifted his foot and ran his hand down Wiley's arm to massage Wiley's elbow.

"Ouch." Holt laughed in sympathy. "I'm sorry. You should start stepping on my foot."

"A little retaliation to keep you on your toes? I like it."

"Har-har." But Holt smiled and his fingers slowed, and then his focus shifted to Wiley's mouth.

Wiley's lips tingled with awareness and since he very much wanted to kiss Holt, he moved sharply back.

Holt let him go.

"It won't even take an hour, but I should get the T-shirt done before the day gets away from me." Wiley yawned and pointed toward the kitchen as he headed to his office. "Help yourself to anything."

"Okay."

Holt sounded almost hurt, but that would be silly. There was nothing to be hurt over.

Wiley fired up his computer and monitors and dug into existing files to patch together a design. He put *Marry Me!* over the CarlaCakes logo, added dates and the episode number, surrounded that in clouds of tiny cupcake-shaped confetti, chose an ombré dye T-shirt base, uploaded the whole thing, sent Carla the info, and called it done.

Then he sat until an hour and fifteen minutes ran out.

He took some deep breaths, set his shoulders, and marched into the living room.

Where he promptly turned gooey-centered and sighed with a longing he didn't fully acknowledge.

All the figurines and village buildings were returned to the shelves, spaces left for those they'd chosen for their not-wedding centerpieces, and those pieces were in a box on the kitchen table wrapped in old washcloths and towels.

Holt was dead asleep on the couch.

The couch was a rare indulgence—he'd searched and searched until he'd found one he could lie on outstretched end to end without his feet or head touching the arms, and double the width with removable back cushions. He'd gladly paid the exorbitant price to have it.

Holt lay curled on his side but fit comfortably, and Wiley was even gladder he'd gotten it.

Wiley grabbed one of Grandma's enormous afghans and was about to toss it over Holt, but he hesitated. Maybe Holt ran even hotter while sleeping and would overheat. Maybe it was weird to think of doing this and then do it and want to tuck Holt in. Maybe he should tiptoe back to his room and fold the laundry and answer the emails he'd neglected since this whole thing started.

A corner of the afghan tumbled from the piled-up fold in Wiley's arms and puddled over Holt's hip.

Holt's eyelids twitched and Wiley held his breath.

The afghan shifted farther and more landed down.

Holt's brow furrowed as he murmured. Wiley stopped breathing.

The afghan enthusiastically answered gravity's call and flumped in ribbons until all Wiley held was the opposite corner.

Holt's mouth lifted and he scooched backward on the couch. He cracked an eye open, peered up at Wiley, and mumbled, "Hmm, hi, nice." Then he reached and insinuated and moved until Wiley was spooned to his front and both of them were more or less under the afghan.

Wiley thought about Carla's list of questions they didn't know and hadn't answered, wondered if their dance by his front door counted as enough practice, and determined that he should pry loose and do anything but this.

Fatigue and warmth and a wonderful sense of security rendered those worries as nothing more than brief flickers that quickly passed as he fell into a deep sleep.

HOLT pulled Wiley closer and sighed contentedly. Wiley was so warm and soft under his hand, and he grinned when Wiley twitched and muscles jumped as the slow rub of his thumb tickled something.

The syrupy intoxication of sleep hadn't fully cleared. Remnants of a heady dream with the man he woke to find in his arms lingered and teased him. He didn't fight past it—he'd had errant fantasies of doing just this for years—it was too good to give up on.

He made a low seeking noise as he feathered kisses at Wiley's nape and then nibbled at Wiley's ear. Wiley was wonderfully responsive, making small noises in return that had his pulse already pounding, arching into his hold and twisting so Holt could kiss the column of Wiley's neck.

Holt tenderly scratched along Wiley's ribs and then pinched Wiley's nipple. He pushed hard enough to feel Wiley's answering pulse in that sensitive spot, and it echoed where he lapped over the fluttering skin in the cup of Wiley's collarbone. Wiley's small noises grew in urgency and strafed Holt like a physical touch.

They tangled but kept on as Wiley turned beneath him and Holt rose onto his palms. He let his knees take his weight and his hips rolled instinctively—he shuddered as Wiley's legs opened just for him and kept him held tight. He had to bow his head and clench his teeth so he didn't rush and miss every last moment to savor.

Wiley's hands ran up his arms. Not as confident as Holt but without hesitation. Holt held still as Wiley explored the width of his shoulders and the texture of his hair and the angle of his spine. Then Wiley's fingertips crept under his waistband, barely there, but the direct contact ignited him.

Holt groaned, wrapped his arms around Wiley, and sat backward, pulling Wiley with him to straddle his lap. He needed to kiss Wiley, to get his hands everywhere, unimpeded.

Wiley tasted sweet and cinnamony. His hair was thick and wavy and slinky between Holt's fingers. His kiss was generous and giving to Holt's demands, and his hands, hooked on Holt's shoulders, felt like fire.

Wiley broke their kiss—to bite at Holt's jaw and a corded tendon straining in his neck—and as Holt cradled Wiley's head, he looked across the room and was jarred to awareness by a framed photo of GB staring at him.

The enormity of what they were doing crashed over him. He summoned every ounce of his strength to stop, to catch Wiley's hands and halt them, to not kiss Wiley a final time as he moved decidedly away.

Wiley's gaze was unfocused and heated, but Holt watched a dawning of similar awareness with dread.

There was no immediate reaction other than Wiley sliding from Holt's lap to the couch. Holt remained painfully immobile. To move would be to gather Wiley back to him, and he couldn't risk that.

"Holt?" Wiley finally asked.

Regret swamped him but he didn't look at Wiley. He didn't want Wiley thinking the regret was over their kiss.

"Wiley, I must apologize. Forgive me."

"No—don't be sorry. That makes it worse somehow."

"Worse?" The implication in that one word shattered Holt, but he forced a smile. Which wasn't fair. He never should have kissed Wiley at all, much less how far he'd pushed.

"Let's not dwell on it. It's not a big deal." Wiley sounded anxious for Holt to accept that and move on.

"Yes, agreed. I get what you mean." Holt wasn't sure he did, but he didn't want to know if it had upset Wiley somehow. Or hadn't been a big deal.

This house and its memories and how he'd always been safe and welcome here plus the wide inviting couch had lulled him. All he'd meant was to have a short nap while Wiley worked. Instead he should have found something to fix or asked outright for a task. He could have read or stopped ignoring the backlog of texts from Kit and Elaine and Janet. No way should he have presumed that welcome was still open to him.

He stood and put the couch cushions and throw pillows back. The afghan was still warm as he folded it and he did so with mindless precision, leaving it in a neat pile at the end of the couch.

Wiley hovered, and it killed Holt that he seemed nervous.

"Should we… it's later than I realized. Do you want some lemonade or need dinner before our lesson?"

Wiley's offer was so ingrained and familiar that Holt had to smile. He retrieved his phone from the coffee table and marveled at the hour. They'd slept the day away.

Holt made a show of flipping through screens and messages and sighed. "I will meet you there, but thank you. Like the T-shirt—I should just get all this," he said and waved the phone about, "attended and resolved sooner than later. That way it's simply done."

"Sure. Makes sense." Wiley moved toward the door, eyes darting to Holt and back several times as they crossed the living room.

As if he was worried Holt would pin him down again or something.

"Did you get the T-shirt all designed, then?" Holt's voice almost cracked but he smiled smoothly. "I'm certain whatever you did, Carla was thrilled."

"You could say that." Wiley opened a screen and held up his phone.

Holt scanned the message from Carla: *38 sold already! wtf! it and this are amazing TY!*

He didn't wait for Wiley to precede him and was mostly out the door when he half turned and paused but didn't say anything.

Wiley waved. "See you later, then. Um, don't forget to eat something." He blinked. "You've mentioned that happens when you get busy, is all."

"So I have and so it does. It's a running bit on the show, even." Mention of the show had Wiley retreating a step into the darkened house. He took the hint. "All right, now I'm going. I will see you at the studio, where I again make another promise not to stomp your feet any more than I can help." He sketched a wave and strode away.

Coward, he thought. *Better part of valor*, he corrected.

WILEY loitered in the stairwell leading to the studio, waiting for Holt.

Not quite waiting *for* so much as waiting so Holt could see he'd gotten here first and was headed upstairs without having waited.

Which meant every passing noise had his heart throttle him as he posed with a foot on the stair above the one he stood on—fourth from the bottom—and swinging his arms as if in midmotion. Only for the outside door not to open and his nerves to unspool and he'd go back to standing on the step with both feet.

It was ridiculous. He was ridiculous.

He'd thought up all manner of recriminations since he'd let Holt leave earlier. After the best sleep he'd had in months nap. After their kiss. After that amazing disaster of a kiss.

Wiley sighed and dropped his face into his hands. He scrubbed it with enough force to bring floaty dots in front of his eyes. Holt probably thought him an even bigger weirdo and left wondering what the huge deal was—it was just a kiss and they were just pretending and what was the harm in getting more used to each other when they weren't under scrutiny.

Sense memory of the span of Holt's hands around his waist and Holt's raspy stubble against his throat and under his tongue and the heat of Holt all around him zinged through Wiley.

Getting used to each other seemed like a bit of an understatement.

That wasn't Wiley's first kiss by any stretch, but it definitely wasn't a kiss among many. Wiley had kissed a few people many times, and in that he'd figured out what he liked and…. Wow. Holt's kisses proved to be everything he liked and then some, and then even more.

He'd wanted so much of that *more*, and then Holt was apologizing and no longer with the kissing, and he had not handled it well at all.

Major understatement.

At least he'd offered lemonade like a champ.

"Hello, Wiley. I worried I was running late, but I'm glad you haven't beaten me here by much," Holt said behind him.

Wiley sighed again. Twenty minutes of readiness to treat Holt with breezy friendliness and douse any lingering worry that the kiss affected him and Holt caught him out flat-footed.

He almost tripped, rolled his eyes, and trudged up the stairs. "I am closer than Fernleaf, so I have an advantage."

"Yes, true. I did get some dinner, thank you for the reminder. I hope you did as well." Holt sounded friendly and casual in the ways Wiley had wanted to.

Wiley huffed and retreated to the far side of the studio.

"Miss Sarah, how are you this evening?" Holt stayed by the door. "I have to confess first thing that we didn't get much practicing in. Our schedule has been pretty demanding."

Holt camera-smiled without glancing his way, and bile burned Wiley's throat.

Sarah arched her eyebrows. "Well. We will do what we can in the time we have." She tapped the floor with her foot, indicating they should join her. "I appreciate your honesty. That's best, as it allows me more accurate assessment of your progress and needs to help you."

Wiley approached Holt and decided he wouldn't take Holt's hand until Holt created the frame, but Holt only stood there.

"Without music to start. I'll count." Sarah moved their arms and hands and built their frame.

Holt's nostrils flared at the clasp of Wiley's hand, but otherwise he didn't react as she inched them closer.

Wiley gazed at the wall past Holt's stupidly tall shoulder and concentrated on Sarah's steady one-step, two-step, one-step, two-step counts.

Sarah stopped counting. "You'd better tell me this as well or we'll get nowhere."

They glanced at each other. Wiley shrugged as if to say, "You think of something," and Holt frowned. The frown created adorable crinkles at Holt's brow, and Wiley grunted for noticing.

"Disagreement over the seating arrangements? Future in-laws horning in with strong opinions on things? Arguing if you should bother packing a formal outfit for your honeymoon?"

Wiley heard in-laws and his mind reeled. He hadn't even thought about that part. How had he not thought about that part? Their frame fell apart and he whipped his head up to stare at Holt wide-eyed, and then burst out laughing at Holt's matching expression.

"Ah, that's already better," Sarah praised. "You two have such natural partner rapport I could tell immediately something was out of sorts. Remember, none of that matters. What matters is that once you've navigated these bumps, you'll be married happily ever after. I'm sure it all seems colossal and stressful, but when you're floating in one another's arms at the reception, you'll have already forgotten all about it."

She grasped their elbows, but they moved without her prompting.

"Yes, good. There you both are. See? Nothing is insurmountable, my dears. Not even this dance."

Holt laughed, a low rumble in his chest that warmed Wiley to the core.

"Keep that in mind." Sarah pushed at the point of their shoulder blades and then their sternums. "Lifting, lifting. Now, inhale deeply, exhale deeply, and find those nice tall backs and square shoulders. We'll do some easy steps around the room to warm up and then add the music."

Wiley slid his hand into Holt's and Holt drew him near and he smiled.

He'd have to confront that whole in-laws alarm still sounding in his mind, but for the moment they had a dance to learn and respite from the bumps, and he took it. What was a little kiss between not-getting-married friends?

Chapter Five

***OH,** I Do!*

I am screaming. Scream-ing!

You are flooding my mentions with the same, and yes, my wonderfuls, I too distinctly heard Holt call his sweetkins "Coy" while they were dancing. I watched it at least ten times and once pausing at each second because I take Science and my duties very very seriously. #yourewelcome

Someone make a gif of it, stat! Better—invent a way to save a video from someone else's social story and give that video unto me.

Coy! Ugh, my heart. They continue to be the worst.

Also flooding my mentions are all sorts of theories on this adorrrrrrrrable nickname and how it's even more adorable to watch Holt say it unguarded to his sweetgums, who then blushes like heck. (Call me old-fashioned, but I am here for Wiley's blushes, m'k?)

One more thing flooding my mentions and kicking up quite the ruckus in the OID Commentariat: that we desperately require a name for Wiley stans and whatever is it going to be?

Isn't it obvious? COYFRIENDS. Hello? #yourewelcome x2

Which begs whatever is a Holt + Wiley portmanteau to do? I leave that one to y'all—I've done my bit for queen and country.

All right, there's old business covered. What's the new goss?

First order, a few right-now-show items. Ohmigosh, the contest they announced! Who but us here ever wanted to be whisked to the wilds of nowheresville more? Stuff the ballot boxes, darlings. I-Doers must represent.

Also, anyone else notice how delightfully distracted Holt is? Gone is our resident type-A overseer. As Kit outlays details and options and all manner of everything, Holt just does this vague smile-and-nod as he steals long glances at Wiley. Who is doing a smidge better at paying attention to anything other than Holt—But Not Much. I don't think either of them care what the wedding entails, aside from you + me = married. It's so romantic and they're so obviously smitten, I could perish.

To that. As this is the season finale and a very-special-episode, they're taking their time with it. Kit upfront secured an extension on their usual film schedule so each and every Layer could get the full everything perfection treatment. It's clear Wilt (oh, oh no)... Hoey (worse, oof)... anyway. It's clear Holt and Wiley are benefiting from the days together. They must be loving having this time in the open with everyone celebrating their upcoming wedding and not having to long-distance a romance on the secret side.

…mentions like this always bring out anti-Coyfriends. You best not brigade, and I will be freezing threads and deleting comments that look to do such. He's not a Yoko, so leave my Coy alone. (Yoko wasn't even a Yoko—blame the band and get over it already!)

Second order. Apparently Odalia is feeling the full force of our fandom powers. We're packing hotels and motels and B and Bs to the brim (protip, you'll have to filter a fifty-mile radius on every booking site search to have a chance), we're scouring local stores and buying up the goods (owners, do nail down anything you want to keep), and we're keeping close tabs on filming. (Hey, stalkers, I appreciate you and your pics, kiss kiss.) Play nice out there.

Say, network bigwigs? We prove once again we're a mighty economic engine! That could be us, but you're playing c-o-y with renewing.

To that, our third order. Noises off and little birdies landing on my shoulder are whispering that this season will be the end, but not because the network pulled the plug. Kit needs his space to shine—not that there's clashes on set, but there are some tensions and odd decisions being made—and I fret even Handyman Holt won't fix this one.

As always: Claws out, drills drawn, and match your BFF heart pendants together—let's get into it in the comments!

HOLT threaded past the shooting setup inside a local restaurant and the milling crew members eating the extra samples the chef had set out, saying good morning as he went to corner Kit. Once he had Kit pinned down, he waved Wiley over.

Wiley had arrived fifteen minutes after him and hadn't avoided him but had fallen into immediate, animated conversation with Elaine, which didn't annoy Holt. There was no reason for annoyance. But he was relieved Wiley finally glanced his way so he could initiate a much-needed confab.

"How is the dance going, darlings?" Kit said as Wiley approached. He lowered his voice. "You should really talk to me more, tell me the updates and where things are."

Wiley's blush momentarily distracted Holt, but not for long. "That's what this is for." He didn't bother saying Kit could go both ways on that street. He checked and saw no one near them but still kept his tone pitched down. "Today is menu tasting, correct? Anything else?"

"I'm going to make you go sit in a cozy romantic setting and choose music for the reception. You won't have to pick more than, say, ten songs. Give the DJ a sense of your preferences." Kit's eyebrows shot up. "Why? Is there something else I don't know about?"

"No. I just wanted to go over the game plan so we know what to expect once we're rolling." Holt tapped Kit's notebook. "Can we have a look at our options and which ones you've circled to lead us to the best choices? And we are settled on this restaurant, correct? You're not surprise dragging us to others?"

Kit huffed in exasperation but complied. "Holty darling. I only huff because it's already in your inbox."

"I liked the sound of the cheese boards, assorted savory hand pies, build-your-own salad, and the miniroasts. Beef and veg options. Everything is family style on the table except two catered salad bars, which seems like a good balance. I've always wanted to try this place, but it's pricey—this one is going well for me." Wiley smiled and looked askance at Holt. "What? I got the emailed list and 'confirm this restaurant made the final cut' too."

Kit draped an arm around Wiley's shoulders. "Always the star pupil. My star. Thank you. At least *one* of you is still taking this seriously."

Holt sighed, but Kit's light kick to the toe of his right shoe made him smile. It was something Kit had done ever since they were little to let Holt know he wasn't actually mad. Especially when their parents had them called on the carpet and Kit was trying to weasel them out of trouble by any means necessary.

"Those all sound fine with me." Holt made a cursory glance at the menu options. Almost everything Kit had circled was something Wiley mentioned. "Are those really fine with you, or did you know they're Kit's idea of the best possible choice?"

"Well, do they really sound fine with you?" Wiley shot back.

"Yeah, this place is known for its hand pies, which I think is great to highlight and support. Can we make sure there are strawberries on the salad bar, and who doesn't like cheese?" Holt caught Wiley's expression—a twinkle in those pretty eyes and the corners of his mouth fighting a smile—and he conceded Wiley's point with a grin. "Here's to nice and easy."

"That's hair coloring, dove. Here's to delectable and delightful," Kit said airily. "Anything else?"

"Will you insist the ten songs we pick be slow dances or…?"

"No, you're off the hook there. I won't torture you with more than your one performed dance." Kit looked from Holt to Wiley. "Seriously, though, how's it going?

Will you totally embarrass me? Yourselves? Find your inner flamenco and run away and join a traveling ballroom troupe? Have you learned anything?"

Holt remembered Sarah's advice from last night. He also remembered waking to find a pliant Wiley in his arms and how even an errant thought of their kiss enflamed him.

"You know, we have." Holt gave Kit the notebook. "Let's meet at Carla's in the morning and compare any other pending notes."

"Yes, of course. Elaine is anxious for more rolls anyway, so I can pick up a bag or two." Kit nodded. "Wiley, just continue being your darling self. Don't overthink or worry. Your off-the-cuff riffs and questions are great. Great flow, great pop of wit without being pert. We don't want to affect either, so don't change a thing. But definitely send up a tiny rescue flare if you're unsure in any moment. 'Kay?"

Wiley regarded Kit with a look Holt could place from when they'd been friends in junior high. Appreciative, a touch awed, and wanting such direct consideration.

Holt grunted. "Yes, do that. I've been paying attention."

"I know." Wiley's expression softened to an inscrutable smile. He nudged Holt. "Thanks."

Kit chuckled indulgently. "Do make it clear if something isn't quite your thing, even if it doesn't make it bad. Per the usual, reserve final decisions until after you've discussed it, have some yeses and maybes. But I'll do the reveal in a talk-time segment with the chef." He let out a pleased breath. "Good! That's settled. Shall we?"

Holt swept his hand in a flourish toward the set.

Wiley let Kit go but waited for Holt. "Thanks also for doing that. I'm kind of getting the hang of this, but it's so much easier establishing stuff from the start."

"It makes it equally easy on me, believe that. And it is only fair to you. This is already outside the norm as it is. Sweating on-the-spot protein main dish choices? No one needs that." Holt's chest expanded when Wiley took his hand.

"Is Janet ever not taking pictures for social media?"

"If Janet is conscious, Janet is on the job." Holt tamped down disappointment. Of course Wiley would be conscientious to notice that and do his part.

"Holt, Wiley? Over here." Elaine gestured at them across the large dining room, where she stood near two marks taped on the floor. "Kit and the chef are going to stand behind the bar, and you'll be on this side. Wiley, is standing okay? It'll make a better shot if Holt's seated and you're at this height."

"I don't mind." Wiley looked everywhere but at Holt.

"You're already perfect as-is, so they know better than to mess with that." Holt said it lightly but didn't tease.

Elaine and Rick laughed. Wiley blushed and snuck a glance at him, so he winked.

"The chef will go over a brief explanation of each dish as staff brings out some tasting plates. Kit might ask for impressions, but feel free to react in the moment. Three cameras for this one. On you two from here, and on the chef and Kit from here." Elaine pointed them out. "And Rick will be on the move. Got it?"

"Ready steady." Holt settled on the stool someone brought over and remained still as Elaine positioned Wiley next to him.

"Can you just… yes, like that," Elaine said as she turned Holt in the seat so he faced center, closer to Wiley than directly across the bar.

He could easily pull Wiley to stand between his legs this way. His thigh brushed Wiley's, and for his sanity he should move it. He didn't.

Elaine moved around as crew styled the bar top and finished the backgrounds, and then the lights came on and makeup did a final pass to buff and powder them.

"Okay, everyone. You should know where we are and what we're doing. At slate we're going to start filming for the episode and the livestream." Elaine counted down on her fingers, and someone ducked in to drop the slate. Then she pointed at Kit.

"Hello, hello—it's one of my favorite layers in the process. The food. The dreamy delectable delightful food." Kit cupped the chef's shoulder and arm and said to the camera, "And speaking of dreamy and delightful, this is Chef Cortez. Chef, meet our grooms, Wiley and Holt."

"Wonderful to meet you, and congratulations. Odalia is so excited to have you boys back filming, and even better, one of you is marrying another local boy." Chef Cortez was stout, dark-haired, with a dark beard and mustache combo, and he flashed a generous smile. He held out a kitchen-scarred square hand. "Call me Pete."

It wasn't often Holt's hand was engulfed, but Pete's firm grip did. "Thank you, Pete. Along with our obvious excitement about what this is for, we're excited to try your food. Didn't I read you introduced the hand pies as an homage to empanadas, but with local ingredients changing seasonally?"

"You did, you did. And thank you for taking the time to read up on Mushroom & Mole. It means a lot to me and my whole staff that, of all the restaurants in town, you chose us to cater your special event."

Holt didn't dwell on not feeling even a twinge of guilt or wrongness at being congratulated and considered a happy couple in front of yet another person they were deceiving. Getting comfortable with the front was part of what made and would keep it successful.

Pete shook Wiley's hand. "You work with Carla at CarlaCakes sometimes, don't you?"

"Yes. Mostly before hours, the Sunday rush, and deliveries." Wiley's smile in answer to Pete's friendliness was quick. "I've been in here a time or two."

That made Holt like Pete even more.

"I knew we knew each other. Good, good. Makes sharing my food with you all the better." Pete turned to Holt. "Maybe Wiley has told you—depending what my menu is wanting week to week, I get breads and rolls from Carla." He patted his belly. "They make the best."

"They do." Holt hadn't known, but that was a good answer nonanswer. He covered Wiley's hand and liked how his engulfed Wiley's.

Holt knew from experience and talking to hosts of other shows that there was a practiced art to appearing fully engaged while the brain was busy on things like shopping lists and planning vacations. But he never learned that art. He hadn't wanted to because he valued what the various couples and local businesses brought to the show and were eager to get from it.

So he listened with sincere pleasure to Pete talk about the parade of dishes they were shown and got to taste, all beautifully presented in single portions, and each with an introduction to a different staff member, sometimes front of house, sometimes the kitchen.

Five years of overpreparation had not prepared him to sit here realizing he really didn't know much about the wedding other than what he and Wiley agreed to, and he didn't mind that one bit.

Aside from the frontloaded research, he hadn't done any work on this episode. Kit had offered the advice to stay fresh. Elaine and the others razzed him for not being on set before they arrived and after they left, nailing down literal and figurative details, and congratulated Wiley for some superpower to keep him out of their way.

Being a participant and not the planner was part of it. But since the announcement upended everything, he hadn't thought about visiting the set or taking on a twelfth project or making sure Kit had it covered. No guilty pangs either.

He watched Wiley eat and smiled. So. Turned out he was definitely ready to leave the show. It was somehow reassuring to see that with such clarity here, doing this.

"These are amazing," Wiley said after another bite of a fresh basil, sundried tomato, and yellow potato hand pie. "This crust is so flaky, I'm jealous."

Pete chortled more than laughed. "My abuela would thank you. It's her recipe."

Wiley's smile turned misty and fond, and Holt tightened his hand over Wiley's. He hadn't realized he'd kept it there, but it looked right between the stack of empty plates and pots of sauces.

"Wiley was raised by his grandmother." Holt smiled at Pete's respectful, understanding nod. "Everything has been amazing, but I think we have a decided favorite in these, don't you?"

"I'm going to have to…." Wiley trailed off and finished by stealing the last of Holt's pie.

Pete chortled again. "I can come up with a very special wedding selection just for you."

"Thank you, Chef." Wiley blushed.

Holt hoped it wasn't from any lingering guilt.

"Now that everyone has had the chance to try Chef Cortez's offerings, I'm sending the affianceds along to marinate on their menu." Kit flicked his fingers their way. "Chef has set up a very special table for you. Off you go."

Holt craned around to follow Elaine's off-camera direction to the far corner of the restaurant, where a booth flickering with low-burning candles and flutes of champagne waited.

"Shall we?" he asked as he slid from the stool. He kept hold of Wiley's hand and his legs opened to brace around Wiley, bodies touching from the spread of Holt's ribs as he breathed to his spread thighs, and they stood a moment staring at each other.

A single sharp clap ripped Holt's attention back to the bar.

Pete nodded sagely. "Now that is happiness," he said with an exaggerated eyebrow raise. "This is a couple who is clearly meant to be."

Kit smiled. "For certain. But first, go and do your work." He shooed them away again.

Holt tugged Wiley toward the booth as Rick followed. Rick stayed, so Holt motioned for Wiley to sit and then folded himself into the booth and left an arm along the back as he settled in. His sitting jostled Wiley enough so Wiley ended up against his side, hand splayed on his chest.

Wiley stayed close but let go to hand Holt a flute and take one for himself.

"To flaky hand pies."

"Cheers." Holt clinked their glasses and sipped instead of downing it like he wanted.

"And, we're out." Rick patted the table. "Great job, guys. We got some good stuff here."

Janet filled the space Rick vacated. "Elaine and company are headed to the kitchen to film the menu reveal. Hang tight in case we need any pickups. After that you both are done for today." She shook a wagging finger at Holt. "Must be so nice. Don't get too used to these hours."

Holt's hand dropped naturally to Wiley's shoulder. "It ain't bad, that's for sure." He finished his champagne and made puppy eyes at Janet while holding out his empty flute.

"I'd say you have more capable hands than most and could just do this, but I get it. Otherwise occupied, super way more important than letting go a few seconds to get your own." She rolled her eyes, but Holt knew her too well to think she actually minded. Janet filled both their glasses and as she headed to the kitchen, yelled, "Ugh, stop being adorable."

"Impossible," Holt shot back and liked it when Wiley laughed.

"So."

"So."

"So, we have champagne and some downtime and this." Wiley set his phone on the table between them and tapped to open a notepad app.

"And this is?"

"Carla's recon. We should at least do the basics, because flowers, outfits, and the cake remain, and that's when these questions really come up." Wiley moved from Holt's side to fold his leg under on the bench seat and cradle his phone to face Holt.

"Let's try rapid-fire."

"I've always liked the lightning round."

"Do you like actual lightning?" Wiley's phone dipped. "That's not on here, but I do."

Holt nodded. "Oh yeah. I love a good storm. The boomier the better."

Wiley grinned. "Nice." He checked his phone. "Okay, here we go. Favorite color? Probably earth tone something."

"I thought I was supposed to rapid-fire answer?" Holt tilted his head. "But that's right. I like woodsy colors best."

"It's the camping and nature thing, I knew it. That and every flannel you've ever worn."

"Every one?"

"Ever."

"Ever?"

"Still." Wiley poked Holt's arm and his woodsy-colored flannel.

Holt had a closetful since he was five and could tell his parents *"like this one."* He'd worn many to help around GB's place. That Wiley thought about it, knew it, speared at his heart.

"Favorite season? I'm sure it's fall, because we agreed it was fall at the barn, where we won't have our wedding reception with the goats and Mr. Pig."

"Right again. As is yours. And—blue. Any and all blues."

Wiley peeped a look at him over the phone. "Yes."

Holt swelled with silly pride. He ticked off on a hand, "You wear a lot of it, you comment on the color of the sky and cornflowers along the road, and your house is decorated with several shades of blue." He shrugged. "The power of deductive reasoning."

"Very observant. Favorite landmark?"

"The Grand Tetons. I think. Maybe. This one's harder—how about mountains."

"I think it's fine to go with landscape instead. I like—"

"The ocean," Holt interrupted, because he wanted to guess and know he was right. "GB took you and Kit to the shore when you dorks were twelve, and you told me all about it. Every day for weeks." He glanced out the big windows with an overlook into trees and rolling hills. "But also around Odalia."

"Yes, also just around Odalia." Wiley smiled and followed Holt's glance. "I'm appreciating it more and more lately. And, wow. You remember that?"

"Every day for weeks makes an impression."

Wiley's blush returned. Holt looked away to refill their champagne but couldn't stop sensing the heat from Wiley's nearness and how Wiley had leaned closer and closer with each exchange. As had he. When he looked back, Wiley's phone was gone.

"That's it? I thought Carla had pages of notes."

"She did, but…." Wiley paused and toyed with the gold rim of his champagne flute. "I don't think we need it."

"I think you're right again." Pleasure filled Holt at how easy and well that went.

"That and Kit seems to be going pretty easy on us. Which, appreciated." Wiley's eyes widened. "I mean, he darn well should. Also—it's all pointless anyway. Same as the mansion and the cutlery and whatever. It's Kit's vision. We're just faking our way through it."

"True enough." Holt drained the bottle into their glasses. "Have you been back to the ocean since?"

"No. It wasn't on purpose—I always wanted to—but somehow making it happen never quite worked out."

"Then that's where you should go."

"Where?"

"The ocean."

"Okay?" Wiley sounded exasperated.

"I mean on the trip you get out of this." As soon as Holt said it, he regretted it.

Wiley didn't quite retreat, but he straightened and set his champagne down. "That's a good idea. I wanted to talk about that, actually."

"Sure. I'm good for bouncing ideas off of. And you should because the sky's more or less the limit, and I can keep you from cheaping out."

"It's not like that. The trip, it's…." Wiley shrugged.

"Do you want to bring someone?" A thought hit Holt hard. "Are you dating someone? Wait, why didn't I ever think to ask if you're dating someone?"

"Of course I'm not," Wiley said, overlapping Holt. He crossed his arms. "As if I'd do all this nonsense to someone I was dating."

"No, that was an insensitive, useless question— you never, ever could do such a thing. I panicked." Holt blinked as Wiley's expression changed to speculative. "Got panicky? Anyway. What about this trip? How can I help? Let me."

Wiley placed a tentative hand on Holt's arm. "I think I want…."

Holt wasn't usually one to have or show any temper, but he could have heaved the empty bottle at Janet when she appeared to woo-hoo at them.

WILEY stared at a place above and to the left of Holt's shoulder and danced the dance of a man rescued before he could make a complete fool of himself.

He would have to bring Janet some cookies tomorrow. For no particular reason.

Sarah corrected something, and Wiley barely reacted to Holt stepping on his foot.

Holt muttered an apology and Wiley nodded, but his usual satisfaction at being way better at this than Holt didn't materialize. He tried to concentrate on posture and helping Holt guide him effortlessly across the floor. Mostly thought about going over the list with Holt and falling into enjoying their easy rapport and almost asking if Holt wanted to join him on the not-honeymoon destination he hadn't even chosen yet.

Thankfully, after Janet interrupted him in the nick of time, the rest of the day accelerated into having to do too many things and be too many places at once for Holt to press him for more. He'd neatly avoided conversation about anything not show-related ever since.

He wouldn't be fortunate enough for Holt to forget, necessarily, but he'd needed the day and its busyness to regain his composure and work out an alternative, reasonable-sounding thing to want instead of a nice trip to the coast somewhere.

It was just…. Pete had been so genuinely happy for them. Kit was so good at acting like it was real and meaningful. Holt was….

Wiley glanced up at Holt's strong jawline with its late-hour stubble darker than his thick light blond hair, his ridiculous silky long eyelashes and unusual eye color, his full lips pursed in earnest concentration.

Holt, he had to admit, was gorgeous. Gorgeous and kind and conscientious and funny and sentimental and huge and sorta kinda maybe perfect.

Which, at the heart of things, was a problem. A big problem. The whole entire problem.

Wiley had gone from palpitations at getting a glimpse of a once-crush to forgetting he'd ever crushed on Kit to realizing he was crushing on Holt despite it being pure folly.

"Sorry," Holt said under his breath.

Wiley shook his head.

"You groaned that time. You usually only make a low hiss." Holt grunted. "One day I won't trod all over you. God, if I do it at the recep—" He stopped and let out a slow breath. "Sorry."

"No biggie. I'm used to it." Wiley didn't try to decide what Holt apologized for any more than he'd give a nebulous answer. "When all this is over, I might just run off and join a ballroom troupe."

Wiley decided it was quite the accomplishment when Holt's grim expression tugged into a smile.

"Yes, much better—stay looser like that, Holt. It will all work much easier if you do." Sarah floated over to them. "You're managing the turns and maintaining a decent frame. I am willing to say you're ready to perform as is. I'd rather you didn't, of course, but there's marked improvement and very much a lovely partner dance in what you're doing."

"I accept that as high praise. Thank you, Miss Sarah." Holt laughed wryly and squeezed Wiley's hand. "And thank you for continuing to so gracefully put up with being battered around the dance floor."

"I hope to get even a smidge more of that out of you before the wedding, but either way, it's almost over. Reprieve is within reach." Sarah clasped her hands together and made the abbreviated bow Wiley had come to recognize signaled the end of a lesson. "Now, it's late, neither of you look rested, and tomorrow is another busy day. Thank you for your efforts, gentlemen, and good night."

"Good night, thank you." Wiley found himself bowing back.

He moved from Holt to grab his things and ignored the coolness that invaded his whole front. His whole self, really. Holt stood waiting at the door and motioned for him to go ahead down the stairs.

"It is almost over, isn't it?" he asked as they walked to the corner where they'd part.

"Yup. Three more 'layers' for us to film and then pulling the emergency exit bar." Holt slowed their pace and studied his hands. "Any thoughts on that? Carla was right—I looked. This episode is going over well, and the livestream apparently has fans and nonfans quite invested in the process and outcome. I don't want to botch it."

"Is that even possible anymore?" Wiley wasn't sure what he was getting at, but yup, he'd asked. "We'll need an actual emergency, or we'll just have to accept it can't end happily for everyone." He hated how close to the bone that cut. "This is why I'm not impulsive or spontaneous. Super easy to start in, super not easy to extricate from."

"We'll stay as loose as we can. I have it on expert authority that helps."

They stopped at the corner and Holt massaged Wiley's shoulders, which got them from up around his ears to not quite pinched in a vee.

"I never expected any of this either, so I'm a novice myself. Although I'm not sure how you could." Holt grinned. "At least that's true for the two of us. I have the feeling our two biggest enablers could bring a wealth of experience and options to the discussion."

"I'll talk to Carla."

"And I will definitely talk to Kit."

Wiley nodded. "Okay. That's a start. Somehow I don't think this part will go as well as realizing we already know each other's favorite color."

"What?"

"What what?"

Holt feathered his fingertip under Wiley's eyes. "They're cloudy with trouble."

"Oh." Wiley had harbored this niggling worry but hadn't thought to bring it up and press the point until now. They were so far in it was real, and he stared the real consequences in the face. "Pete and the mansion owners and everyone else—they'll all get paid, won't they? And positive press? This is our lie, not theirs."

"Sweet Wiley," Holt said so quietly it almost got lost in the rising breeze. "Every vendor, every local we hire temp, every one of our crew. Every cent they're owed. I went over it with Kit and legal to be sure as soon as we hatched this scheme." His stern expression more than his words told Wiley it was true.

"Oh, oh good." Wiley sighed with relief and sagged into Holt. "Not that I didn't think you would, but what if there was some contract fine print I was messing up? I couldn't stand that."

"Me either. So don't worry about it again." Holt dragged his thumb along Wiley's neck, and his eyes got hooded. "We will figure something out. Something that might not be happy for everyone but won't be a total disaster. I promise."

"Me too," Wiley whispered.

Holt nodded jerkily and then kissed Wiley, short and hard. "Good night, Coy," he rumbled and then pulled back sharply to charge across the street and stride away.

Wiley walked a much more subdued pace home, and as he unlocked the door he thought how, if Holt had asked if he wanted company, he'd have invited Holt in.

Chapter Six

HOLT ducked into the vestibule of their location for the day and shook rain from his hair and shoulders.

"Get in here so we can fix that," Keelie said while opening the door.

"Yes, ma'am." Holt followed her to a line of chairs, and she had the hair dryer on before his butt was in the seat.

"One day I'll convince you to carry an umbrella." She fluffed and combed and included his damp shirt.

"Probably not. Maybe I just like you fussing over me too much." He grinned and she turned the hair dryer to blast his face and then kept working.

He kept his eyes closed and mentally reviewed the notes for today's shoot. Flowers. Boutonnieres, swags for the aisle chairs and adorning the porches at the mansion, centerpiece accents, and a large arrangement for the guest book and find-your-seat table.

Late last night Holt made sure to read Kit's email. It included plenty of direction without telling them exactly what to pick.

"Wiley? Right next to your man, if you please," Keelie called over the hum of the hair dryer and general noise in the room.

"Morning." Wiley sounded breathless.

Holt had to get a look.

He turned despite Keelie's hold on his head and smiled.

Wiley's eyelashes were spiky with moisture, and his thick hair was plastered down. Rivulets ran down his cheeks and neck, and Holt couldn't resist touching, following their course on Wiley's skin.

"Morning. Great timing on that downpour, eh?" *Stay loose*, he thought, and leaned in to kiss Wiley, natural as anything.

Wiley returned the kiss. Enough to appear mutual, not so much to go overboard, plenty to get Holt's blood heated.

He shifted in the chair, and Keelie turned the hair dryer away.

"Need a moment?" she asked tartly.

"No," he choked. He cleared his throat and said more clearly, "No."

She um-hummed knowingly and finished fluffing and combing and then moved on to Wiley.

Lars appeared in her place and made quick work of doing Holt's camera makeup "no-makeup look."

Kit joined them next, and as soon as Lars was gone, scooted a chair crowded to theirs, sat poised on the edge, and said, "Questions, comments, did you read what I sent?"

"No, why are we here instead of a florist, and yes." Holt removed the tissue Lars had stuck in his collar and wadded it in his hand. Without thinking he held his palm out for Wiley's and added it to the wad.

"You two are bonding so nicely and it shows so well on camera." Kit smiled in an according-to-plan expression Holt knew well, and got out his notebook. "If you do have any, here's my notes. We're here because I wanted to have the fun of making a pop-up store—after we're through, we're opening this up to the masses and they can come in and buy all the samples and examples, terribly fun and an amazing idea, right? And amazing, thank you, I'm bowled over."

Kit opened his notebook to a tabbed section and gave it to Wiley. "I know you read the email, dearest, but give a look-see and poke me if you need."

"That actually is a good idea. I always hated the waste from some segments." Holt drummed his fingers on his thigh. "That also explains why so many people were milling around on Main Street in the rain hours before anything opens."

"It came to me like a bolt of genius! Which, it is. It's something I should do again, somehow," Kit said leadingly but then waved a dismissive hand. "Anyway, I told Todd and Regina not to bring anything they want to have a chance of taking back to the shop with them." He surveyed the cavernous, bricked space. "We'll have to tell people the structural pillars aren't for sale, so please don't hacksaw and drag them away."

The structural pillars formed a dignified regiment that defined the main room, standing in a staggered grid of twelve rising to what was probably a twenty-foot ceiling. The once pristine white paint had cracked and peeled, but their lines remained plumb and true.

"Wasn't this Sinclair Hardware once upon a time?" Holt remembered counting the pillars and marveling at tiny bins filled with nuts and bolts and nails and screws as his father hunted up a replacement pull for a kitchen drawer or a latch for the garage door. The dark-patina wood floor had creaked even when he was a kid.

"It was. You used to beg Dad to come here so you could count washers or whatever. It was well past its prime then but still impressive." Kit *tsk*ed. "Sad what's happened, even if we are brightening it for the day."

A bubble of righteous indignation rose in Holt's chest. "Is it just going to be allowed to rot away?"

"Old man Sinclair—who was really the original old man Sinclair's grandson—passed away before any decisions about selling or someone else taking over were made." Wiley frowned. "I think the city has ownership at this point. Tax default. It's the biggest storefront on Main Street, so rent or purchase would be steep, but the Restore Downtown Commission won't let it be subdivided, so no one knows what to do with it."

"I'm sure someone will think of something." Kit stood and brushed nonexistent dust from his slim pale puce suit. "Someone very optimistic and with a lot of money and can-do elbow grease to burn." He pulled a face. "Awful. Wiley—come with me, darling. Let's peruse the bevy of floral beauts awaiting you so you're primed and ready. Holt, humor me and read my notes, and then do come join us."

He didn't have much choice in taking the notebook Kit thrust at him, but he duly went over Kit's bullet lists and arrows pointing to next thoughts and ideas and circled callouts and asides. Pictures clipped from magazines were washi taped here and there alongside Kit's sketches and paint chips arrayed to show a color story.

Kit could be a diva and flighty and even terrible, but Kit also meant business about getting the weddings he planned right. Even if the wedding was fake.

Holt sought Wiley out and relaxed just from finding him among the hubbub and watching him bury his face in a bouquet of flowers.

There was a lot—too much—that didn't seem fake anymore. Last night, on the verge of asking if he could walk Wiley home and into the house and then to bed, had been entirely too real.

Blame it on a combination of stress and being thrown together and how Wiley's concern no one else suffer fallout had made his heart turn over.

Holt snapped the notebook shut and walked it to the pile of Kit's things at the command center area set up at the front of the room. He gazed out the dirty front window, and Kit's dismissive comments about the store rattled in his mind.

Aside from the pillars, the only original architecture still intact was the massive oak counter and floor-to-ceiling bins behind it, seemingly pulled directly from an Old West movie's mercantile store. Production and the florists had stuffed the bins to overflowing, with flower bundles in some and vases representing Kit's color story in others. The countertop had a hinge-top access. Holt had longed to try it the moment he'd discovered it, trailing his dad around the store, but of course it had been off-limits.

No more.

He went directly to it, lifted it up, and stepped through.

Letting it drop again required twisting to change his hold. The hinges protested and the gate didn't quite fit in its ogee anymore. Definitely not as cool as he'd once imagined. If this were his, he'd consider removing it or devising a smoother transition with lighter weight wood and hidden hydraulics.

"Ben?" Holt didn't have to yell—he had a certain tone he'd learned cut through the noise and got the attention he needed.

Ben trotted over and tugged his jangling tool belt tighter to his slim waist. "Hey, man, what's up?" He high-five-hugged Holt over the counter. Ben was fair and his cheeks were always pink, but exertion made them red. "It's hard work being in charge with you taking it easy, all too busy getting married to do your job."

Holt grinned. "Aww, we both know this episode is in great hands with you." He lifted the gate and raised an eyebrow meaningfully.

"A tragedy." Ben scowled, his thinking face. "I'm on it. Don't think we have time for good as new, but it won't do that on film at least."

"More than enough. Thanks, Ben."

Ben clicked his tongue and went in search of whatever that thinking face decided was needed.

Kit and Wiley were absorbed in conversation, and rather than acknowledge a twinge of dislike he couldn't quite pin down, Holt wandered around the old store. The line-leaded windows over the office at the back were fine, but their caulk and sashes looked a puff of wind away from collapsing. The office interior was worse. He could tell the team had abated evident mildew so they could film in here and then have the public in to shop, but if anyone was going to take this place on, digging down to and removing the source would be the first job.

He didn't dare test the stairs leading to the half-story loft that overlooked the main floor. He wouldn't even trust Wiley on them.

Holt tested one with his foot. It cracked alarmingly, and the whole structure moved. Most definitely would not trust Wiley to them.

"Ben?"

Ben appeared, pencil stuck behind an ear and laden with an assembled counter hinge-top repair kit. Holt would miss him. They thought alike and had become good buddies over the years.

"Yo."

"Please make sure this—" Holt stepped back so he could gesture at the entirety of the staircase and several feet out for good measure. "—is both blocked off and has someone here to make sure no one can access it while the pop-up is open."

"On it again." Ben shook his head sadly. "The tragedies compound."

"They sure do," Holt muttered as he finished his inspection of the once grand hardware store.

"Holty? Ready, then?" Kit waved him to the counter. "Wiley is set on flowers, so don't even worry about having a say."

His light quip sent a rising *ooooooh* through the crew as they worked.

"Fine with me. Whatever Wiley wants and makes him happy is what makes me happy." Holt let himself pull Wiley to him, and he wanted to kiss Wiley's forehead and nose and the corner of Wiley's mouth—not because of any expectation or audience—so he did.

The *ooh* turned into *awwwww* and kissy sounds.

"Ugh, can it," Holt grumped but couldn't manage to sound annoyed. He turned and headed to the counter setup and kept Wiley close to him.

"It's just good seeing you so happy, boss. I mean, it would have been nice to know about it before the rest of the world." Ben raised his voice over a general murmur of agreement. "I know, I know, it was casual and then suddenly not and then absolute cone-of-silence time so no one spoiled anything." He dropped the counter flap and waggled his brows as it swung smoothly into place. "But you could have trusted us—not with your privacy but a very special episode? Hell yeah."

People whistled and a few clapped.

Holt got onto the stool Elaine pointed out and snagged Ben's arm as he tried to retreat.

"I'm going to commend your repair job there and leave it at that." Holt leaned in. "Thanks, bud."

Ben saluted him and Wiley. "It's snack time. Someone let me know when they're wrapped so I can deal with the menace of those stairs."

Makeup freshened, lights on, and then Elaine called places. Their blocking echoed the menu tasting, Holt seated this time to Wiley's right and Wiley standing on one side of the counter, Kit and Todd and Regina on the other.

The flower choosing went by in a blur. Holt fought to make appropriate noises and maintain interest, but his attention wandered to critically assess various aspects and issues in the crumbling store, and whatever focus he had remaining seemed riveted to the spot where Wiley's hip rubbed against his waist.

He had a vague impression of pearly, pale colors—not unlike Kit's suit, tie, and pocket square, something

Kit often did—and he managed to agree peonies created impact.

"What if the enormous guestbook table arrangement is bursting and cascading all over, like springtime in a vase. No, forget vase. A veritable bathtub of an urn. And then every other arrangement will take two flowers from the big bouquet and orchestrate this divine harmony of blousy way-too-much goodness leading to elegant restraint." Kit propped his chin on closed fists, elbows on the counter. "Yes?"

Regina gasped in approval. Todd slid a vase full of peonies closer to Kit.

"I...." Holt swallowed past dryness as he scrambled for a reply and patted the small of Wiley's back. "I like that."

When had he moved his hand to the small of Wiley's back?

"And I like the drama on the table and the restraint on our lapel."

Everyone shared a camera-chuckle at Wiley's quip, and then he took hold of a peony stem.

"May I?"

"Be my guest." Todd pulled it from the vase and handed it over.

Wiley pinched it near the blossom and stuck it in one of Holt's buttonholes. "Perfect."

"No, darling, you two," Kit said and gave Wiley and then the camera a broad look. "Stunning—maybe only that, then. We'll have to confab and decide!" He turned to the others. "Thank you so much, Regina and Todd, for blessing us with your beautiful blossoms. It's like floating on magical clouds in here, everyone. Ugh, so great."

"Well, thank you, Kit. And Holt and Wiley. This is truly our pleasure." Regina plucked another peony from the vase and handed it to Wiley.

Todd reached for a sprig of jasmine and gave it to Kit. "But this for you, I think."

"Right again." Kit breathed deeply. "Gorgeous." He set the sprig down and then started gathering flowers, as if to plan a bouquet. "I can't wait to finalize the designs and see them in their glory at the reception."

Regina and Todd made similarly busy, while Holt and Wiley held still. Rick zoomed in on Kit placing and zhuzhing flowers in a vase.

"And we're clear. Awesome stuff, everyone." Elaine stepped in and flattened her hands on the counter. "We'll have a look, see if there's anything to retake, but I think we're good."

Wiley made a musing noise. "You know, there haven't been many retakes, but I expected them. Is that unusual?"

"Not super-duper such for a program like this. If there were big blunders we'd go again, but Holt and Kit are consummate pros and you're holding your own, so you've given us mostly clean footage to work with." Elaine spread her hands. "That and we're trying to keep it as authentic-seeming as possible, since viewers are getting the insider and behind-the-scenes peeks on the livestreams. If it's too polished in the episode, they'll start to wonder about things we don't want them wondering about."

"Like authenticity of the other episodes." Wiley nodded. "Got it."

"Pretty much." Elaine flopped her binder open on the counter and jabbed at the schedule with the soft stylus of her pen. "We're also fighting time. We have to have this cut, edited, and in the can by your wedding day."

"Really." Holt glanced at Kit. "And why is that?"

Elaine shot a puzzled look at him. "Because your episode is going to premiere without the whole wedding part, and then you'll be getting married live immediately after?"

"Was this in another email of Kit's I didn't read?" Holt asked mildly. It took some restraint.

"Holty, my favorite eldest brother, it was in the discussion we had on the first day." Kit widened his eyes meaningfully. "You know when… I did say it had been set in advance to have some parts aired live."

"I guess it didn't sink in the wedding would be live." He recalled livestream and behind the scenes being said but not anything else. "Why does this seem like new information to me?"

"You're understandably distracted and anxious to cross the finish line here. Elaine and I have handled the bits and pieces, and it's gone fine." Kit patted Holt's hand that had curled into a fist on the counter. "Not much longer."

"And too much to do in it. Gents, I'll see you soon. Unless you hear from me, we're solid on today's shoot, and I have the feeling we're solid. And Kit—don't forget we have some confession-booth stuff. I thought doing it with the floral backdrop here would be great." Elaine gathered her binder and hustled off.

"Confession sounds like a good idea." Holt pinned Kit with a look. "We need to talk."

"I know. But what could I say around Elaine?" Kit reached over and patted Wiley's hand while still patting Holt's. "We can talk in the morning at the bakery. But babes, we're golden. I'm looking out for you."

"By planning a live ceremony? How do we extricate ourselves from a live event there's not even any invitations to or was ever going to happen?" Wiley narrowed his eyes. "I don't remember that either, exactly. Or any email Holt didn't read with that in it."

"Don't panic, Wiles. And don't give me that look either. I know you in studious, follow-the-rules-only mode. I've thought our way all the way around and through this. Like always. You know there's no one better at finding the best-case and making it appear the only ever triumph." Kit nodded confidently, and then he leaned forward. "This part wasn't entirely my idea. Network brass maneuvered me into this more than I could completely countermand, so believe and trust this is the toned-down version of what they envisioned to get a ratings and advertiser tie-in bonanza."

Holt pinched the bridge of his nose. "I feel this could have been shared. At, like, any time."

"And don't you be imperious and so very reasonable." Kit blinked rapidly and looked away. "You're under enough strain as it is, and I'm trying to prevent any more getting heaped on your plate, in part because the less stressed, the more natural you are on camera. Even real couples find this stretch of cooing over endless loops of my layers difficult, and I'm determined to save you from as much of the drudgery as possible by heavy lifting this non-wedding that comes to an in-everyone's-best-interests conclusion." He looked back at them, eyes shiny with moisture. "Okay? And now see, I'm having to have an emotion. How dare. But I also have a plan, and this is going to plan, and we'll come out smelling like, well…." He gestured dramatically. "Take your pick."

Holt had a sensitive and well-calibrated bullshit meter when it came to Kit. What was theatrics, what could be safely ignored, what had to be nipped in the bud, and what fell in the middle.

This—Kit having a plan and working them toward it—was the truth.

Holt was chagrined that surprised him.

"Is there anything else?" Wiley twirled the peony he still held. "And I don't mean that you're thinking complementing suits for us and not tuxes."

Kit chewed his lip and then leaned in again. "Invitations have gone out."

"To who?" Holt crossed his arms, started to crush the giant blossom in his shirt, and had to uncross them.

"Again—unavoidable but handled. As heavily as I've leaned on the whole it-was-a-secret-until-the-reveal narrative, we can't undo that it's known to the whole world, since you announced not only your engagement but plans to marry." Kit held up a staying hand. "Ah, no. Listen. Unavoidable because it was part of the live ceremony package idea. There's a fan contest attached, so they can win and attend as my plus-one, done that way so that's on me and I'm dealing with it. Otherwise, nothing overboard, but this is why I'm chugging full speed on whipping up the greatest reception ever so there's a rocking party we can drown our non-sorrows in after you all don't get married as planned."

"Anything else, else?" Wiley was pale but composed.

"Nope." Kit exhaled loudly. "Really, you two mopes, I've gotten you this far. I will get you the rest of the way and exactly where you belong, and you'll feel silly we ever had this conversation, because the end result will be everything you said you wanted out of this and more."

Holt wasn't sure that was true, but he could tell Kit believed it.

"Kit?" Elaine got near enough so she didn't have to yell. "We're ready for confessional booth. You two are good to go. Thanks for your work today."

"Be there in a shake." Kit smiled and waved until Elaine turned back around. "Just keep doing like you're doing. Learn the dance, let me handle the rest. And stay off social media—it'll all get too much in your heads otherwise." He wagged a finger, made a quick selection of several flowers, and walked away.

"Tomorrow morning at the bakery," Holt called after Kit. He removed the peony from his buttonhole and tossed it on the counter with a sigh. "What a morning."

"I feel like we've been doing this forever and it's been a whirlwind at the same time."

"I convinced myself going through the motions and only the motions would do. I shouldn't have gotten lax about my usual duties. No one in production would think it odd I'd treat my own wedding the same as the rest, more so even, ready to attend any needed fix at a moment's notice. I am sorry."

Holt didn't add how comfortable he'd gotten in the endless loop of seeing Wiley every day, filming a segment with most of his attention on making sure Wiley was fine and they looked the part, and stomping Wiley's nimble feet before parting at the corner in anticipation of doing it all again the next day. So comfortable it hadn't seemed important to pay attention to the details.

"You take too much on as somehow your responsibility, and it's not. Don't be sorry. I could have been scouring the internet and sussed all this out but, well…. Pretending to be getting married is exhausting." Wiley drooped into Holt. "Especially with Kit in charge."

He caught Wiley into him and tucked Wiley's head under his chin.

"What's left?"

"Tuxes—or suits it seems—and the cake." Holt combed Wiley's hair with a hand. "I think the suit fitting is when you get your surprise non-honeymoon wardrobe."

Wiley shook his head. "I told Kit I didn't want it. I like my clothes and my closet is small and it would add hours to our filming day, and I thought, no." He huffed a laugh.

"No makeover fancy wardrobe and maybe a trip to the coast for you, not having fixed one damn thing for me, there's a contest and packs of fans in town, invites sent out, place-settings we both hate, and we're still going to dance lessons like we'll be graded on it." Holt snickered. "We're doing great."

"So great."

"At least I got to see this old place again."

"You did always like it most about Odalia. That and Grandma's cookies." Wiley pressed closer in. "I'm going to nap, okay? Just… wake me if there's an emergency."

Holt should laugh but push Wiley away and go track Kit down, get a handle on the details and every other thing he'd neglected. He should give Wiley a minute's respite and then say all right, let's go somewhere to strategize. He should stop mooning over the store not yet lost to decay and the feel of Wiley in his arms as the familiar rhythm and noises of production worked around them.

He didn't.

"WE'LL take five, and then one more run-through and we are finished for tonight." Sarah paused the music and cued it back to their song. "I'm staying over here to observe, so don't forget posture and frame and taking it gently into the turns."

Wiley exhaled and shook his arms and hips.

"You're a bit, I don't know, almost nervous." Holt laid his hands on Wiley's shoulders. "Is everything Kit finally had to tell us getting to you?"

"No." At Holt's look he added, "Honestly. Yes, it was a lot to take in. And I admit that I decided I didn't have to take it all in because that's out of my hands anyway, so why overload. Freaking out won't make this any easier. But I'm still doing okay."

"Not a bad approach. No regrets?" Holt rubbed his thumbs up and down Wiley's neck. "Or at least, regrets you can live with?"

Wiley suppressed a shiver. "I think that's a fair assessment." He stared at Holt's chest, and something clicked inside as he made up his mind.

"What's that?"

"That?" Wiley frowned up at Holt.

Holt tapped his forehead. "That that, whatever just happened in here."

"Nothing?" Wiley said coolly and then immediately ruined it by adding, "How could you tell?"

"We're to the point we don't need to cram study Carla's list, remember?" Holt's eyes twinkled and he leaned forward.

Wiley tipped his chin in answer and his mouth tingled.

Holt's hands tightened.

Wiley's breath caught, and then Holt's brows shot up and he let go to chase the awful sound his phone was making.

"Miss Sarah, that's the only-if-it's-on-fire ringtone," Holt explained as he crossed the dance floor and picked it up.

Wiley's heart stuck in his throat. Had they been discovered? Exposed? Could it be the escape they needed for not marrying before they got closer to the finale of not marrying, and why did the thought of that twist Wiley's heart the most?

Holt read something as he walked back to Wiley, and Sarah came to join them.

"It's not Kit or a disaster. Everything is still just as it should be."

"Except with whoever sent you an it's-on-fire series of texts."

"Ben has a conundrum." Holt's grin went from palpable relief to near glee. "He's asking if I can please go help fix something."

"Well, then go." Wiley turned to Sarah. "That is, with your permission."

"I think if I insisted we run the dance a final time tonight, your foot would suffer even more than usual with Holt's mind elsewhere." She smiled. "Wiley, get some rest. Holt, good luck with your firefighting, and if it takes you late into tonight, sleep in tomorrow."

"Thank you." Holt kissed Sarah on the cheek.

She arched one delicate eyebrow but didn't complain.

"And thank you," Holt said in a deeper register and kissed Wiley on the mouth. Then he gathered the rest of his things and rushed away.

As Wiley retrieved his own phone, he smiled at Holt's newly arrived text.

See you tomorrow early at the bakery. We've got this.

"Good night," he all but yawned at Sarah as she ushered him out.

"After all of this is over, you should consider coming here for classes." Sarah inclined her head. "You have excellent movement quality and instincts and are certainly making Holt a better partner for it."

"You know, I just might. Thank you." Wiley waved and plodded down the stairs without any movement quality.

It wasn't a bad idea. He'd have to do something to fill the hours and days after this craziness overturned and then left his life. He didn't think helping Carla and designing freelance would cut it anymore.

He got to the corner and stood there staring in the direction of Fernleaf. Holt's eager mood lift at being summoned made him smile and tore a groan of pure frustration from him. He'd either had a lucky narrow escape or had the worst stroke of fortune.

Holt had been right; something had happened inside him. That click.

He'd decided to ask Holt to come home with him tonight.

Chapter Seven

OH, *I Do!*

I'm starting with getting preachy, which I resent even has to happen but. But! Little Odalia PD has released a statement for roving fans to stop climbing on the statue of the town founder and that there's been a rash of incidental—but very real—burglaries in the area since filming started and for residents to be "aware and prepared."

Also, I am releasing a separate statement to share to all the socials that I've seen fans post photos of Wiley's house and some candids of Wiley and Holt about town and, no. Nope. This is not cool. Don't make me get my squirt bottle. Be enthusiastic, not creepy!

Absolutely stop climbing onto the plinth to get a selfie with the founder. I realize it's become ~a thing~

and someone will bust into the comments to defend it, but one, no, and two, no. I'm not absolutely convinced it's a fan-involved crime spree, because we're just not about that. But, as Chief Wilkins rightly said, be aware and prepared out there. And pass your tips on to the Odalia PD if you see anything sus.

Thus closes my PSA. Thank you.

So, what's the what otherwise? The wedding is almost here, and *I* have butterflies. I also have my outfit selected, on-theme snacks ready to go, and champagne on the chill. I can't wait for us to pick apart every detail together, live.

Speaking of, watching the livestream shows a very different Holt. This Holt, all cute and besotted, has me feeling quite the identity crisis. What if I'm—gasp—turning into a Holster?

It's just... the pictures and clips Holt posts from their dance lessons are total adorbs time, and speaking of again, who else had to lie down after seeing that picture of Holt catching a catnap propped on Wiley's dear head while Wiley catnapped on his chest, all surrounded by gorgeous flowers?

They disgust me.

I might have printed and framed it.

The contest winner is about to be announced, and full disclosure, I'm not eligible because I'm media and so I leave it to one of you OID devotees to snag it and provide the intel. Don't let me down!

Not a lot of goss to report. Things are getting locked down over there, but there's no grumblings or rumblings either, which is a good sign. It feels like the bigwigs are really happy with this format and special episode, but I also can't shake feeling like they're kinda making it up as they go along. Just me? hm.

As always: Claws out and drills drawn, let's get into it in the comments!

"**YOU** look terrible. I'm making you toast. Toast fixes almost everything."

Wiley laid his head on the counter and groaned. "We're up to three years. It's been three years since you dragged me to the park, and instead of reacting like a sane person, I said 'oh sure okay I'll pretend to be getting married on TV, no problem.'"

"Four, at least. Time is exponential when you're pretending to get married on TV."

Carla set something down and the vibrations tickled Wiley's head. He'd heard that distinctive sound on this countertop enough to make a noise of appreciation and reach for the mug of coffee and drag it closer without looking.

"Five." Wiley hunched over the cup and slurped coffee as Carla buttered his toast. He inhaled three pieces and had a bite of a fourth before he paused. "Okay, so I was hungry."

"Did you forget to eat last night? Or lie down thinking you'd get up any minute and shower, then eat, but instead wake up with your alarm this morning?"

Wiley polished off the toast. "Exactly that."

Carla read his longing glance at the empty plate and cut several more slices of bread.

"Did you get an invitation? To my non-wedding?"

Carla's vigorous slicing slowed. "It wasn't phrased that way, natch, but I did."

"Were you going to tell me about that? Like, didn't you think it was worth mentioning that invitations were sent for a wedding that won't be happening?"

She set the slices to take their spin in the industrial toaster and wiped her hands on her apron. "I assumed you knew or maybe one of you was messing with me. It arrived a few days ago. They're nice," she added almost apologetically. "Here."

Carla ducked into the kitchen and returned with a thick envelope, which she handed to Wiley.

He held it like it might bite.

Carla's bakery address was printed on gray paper with a rose-gold sheen. Inside, the envelope was lined with darker rose-gold foil with the invitation tucked in a smaller vellum envelope. The invitation was flat and embossed and ornate and matched the items he could kind of recall from their décor segment.

Holt's full name and his full name in looping, intertwining script dominated the design.

Dread, a bit of defeat, and absolute undeniable longing pooled in Wiley's gut.

"This seems... way more official than I was prepared for."

"I think that sums up pretty much everything so far." Carla dropped the washcloth she halfheartedly had been pushing around and drew a stool to her side of the counter. "I never should have pestered you about your year of mostly-no yes."

"You couldn't know it'd lead to this." Wiley pictured Holt. "It's okay. Really."

"Is it?" Carla tilted her head. "I've been wondering, and you don't get that dopey look easily."

"No," Wiley said with enough force to stop her before she got further.

"No what?" Holt appeared in the kitchen doorway with a steaming mug of coffee in one hand and a day-old danish in the other. "Whatever it was, it sounded like you meant it."

Wiley tried but couldn't stop smiling at seeing Holt and Holt's endearing comfort at the bakery. Holt settled onto the stool next to him and grinned back.

"Hi."

"Morning." The way Holt sat put them too close together, but Wiley didn't move. "Carla got this." He slid the invitation over.

Holt shoved the danish in his mouth and inspected the envelopes and invite. "That's quite something," he said through a disappearing bite and swallowed. "And that leads you to no?"

"No. I mean, it does, yes, but not no to that. It's just everyone is apologizing and taking responsibility for me getting into this when I got me into this. Maybe I didn't have the full scope, but I certainly was aware of the stakes when I agreed, and I've held up my end. And I want credit for that." Wiley carefully put the invitation into its vellum envelope and that back into the larger envelope. "Credit isn't quite the right word. This fake wedding has been good for me, and I'm still not sorry I said yes."

"How so?"

Wiley looked at Holt and smiled. After a moment he realized that couldn't be his whole answer.

"It forced me out of my rut, not by taking some big lavish trip but how it jolted me from inertia, here." Wiley swept his arm behind him toward the bank of windows. "And I've rediscovered how much I like Odalia, and being a baking assistant, that I show promise at ballroom dancing, that I'm not stuck here."

"You're still taking the trip, though, aren't you?" Carla raised her hands when Holt and Wiley stared at her.

"What? Life epiphanies are great and all, but he's earned it and should have some fun and relaxation after this."

"And then some." Holt turned to Wiley. "Book one of those private tropical cabanas that are way out on the water. Then it's all ocean all the time."

"I'll add it to the list. I still haven't decided." Wiley finished his coffee and snagged the pot to refill everyone's mug. "I do think I want to renovate the kitchen, but otherwise, saying yes has gone pretty well."

"As soon as Kit gets here, we'll figure out an exit strategy to keep it that way." Holt checked his phone. "If he doesn't answer my text, I'll call him in a minute."

Wiley ate more toast and tried not to be glum.

"We can get a start." Carla reached under the counter and pulled out her notebook.

"I'm starting to think I need to keep one of these." Wiley pulled it to him and flicked the pages. "Notebook, planner, binder. Think of all the stickers I could buy."

"I've never kept one either. I do okay." Holt's phone chirped and he looked at it and grunted. "Kit is unavoidably delayed and won't make it but says whatever we come up with he's behind 100 percent, unless it's totally wrong, and he'll go over the plan later for necessary tweaks."

"Okay, so we'll start and finish a plan." Carla tugged her notebook back and flipped to a blank page. "First we should establish what and we can work back to why. From what I've read online, I think going with delaying the wedding versus outright canceling will cause way less grief."

Unexpected noise from the kitchen made all three snap to attention at once.

Ben stopped short as he walked in. "Hello, good morning." There was a certain expectation in his arrival, in coming through the back unannounced at this hour, which made him seem quite familiar with the bakery. "Am I interrupting something?"

Wiley glanced at Carla, who blushed crimson with her arms folded on the closed notebook. The blush wasn't guilt or nerves from almost getting caught scheming.

"Or we can table the discussion for later." He raised an eyebrow and murmured, "Well, well, well."

Carla shushed him and stowed the notebook. "I have your rolls and bear claw order ready."

"And breakfast still?" Ben asked hopefully. "If that's all right for me to join in."

"Of course." Carla widened her eyes at Wiley and ignored Holt's growing grin. "Let me get you a stool. Who wants more toast?"

HOLT drummed his fingers on the armchair in Odalia's single, small but refined, actual haberdashery and tried not to show his impatience.

He had endured being shoved into and trotted out in a dark blue trim-fitting suit, a process he hated, but Wiley's roaming gaze and obvious appreciation made it more than worthwhile for once.

Waiting on Wiley's turn and dreading the next two rounds he'd go through proved less rewarding.

"Are we prepared?" Kit asked as he drew the curtain back from the dressing room. "I'm going to say no. Wiley, come on out and show yourself off."

Wiley appeared, and Holt's impatience evaporated. Everything evaporated except for Wiley, handsome and shy and seeking out Holt's eyes.

Holt stood without knowing he had and was two wide steps toward Wiley when he realized it and stopped.

Then he didn't do anything but stand there and stare as Wiley's shyness slowly broke into a pleased grin.

"And?" Kit prompted.

"Stunning." Holt couldn't look away to answer.

Kit pressed Wiley's lapels and straightened the hang of his jacket. "Dark blue with light accents on you and light gray with dark accents on him. Wiley's idea, and a fine one." He moved away and cast a critical eye over Wiley. "Give us a twirl."

Wiley dutifully twirled. Holt dutifully noticed the fit of Wiley's pants at the bulge and butt.

Holt swallowed and discreetly adjusted.

"Marvelous. You can go take that off. We are done here," Kit declared.

Holt leveled Kit with a look. "Not three?"

"Nope. These are it." Kit waved imperiously. "Sometimes, the powerful drama of a single strong reveal is better than any cavalcade of options followed by a cliffhanger."

Holt liked to think he more often than not knew when it was better not to argue. This was definitely nothing to argue about.

Kit walk-and-talked the camera to the dressing room and reappeared, their contrasting pocket squares in hand, to walk-and-talk to Sven, the stooped tailor with his ring of white hair and keen gaze, and Sven's daughter Helene, hovering in readiness to assist.

"Psst." Holt slipped past the dressing room curtains and the sharp turn that acted as another visual baffle into the open dressing room.

Wiley had his head and both upraised arms in his shirt and the lines of his hips exposed by the undone fly of his jeans. His abdomen rippled as he wriggled into the shirt and then his head appeared, hair mussed, and somehow him twisting to tuck in his shirt was the sexiest part of all.

"I was just going to say, uh." Holt coughed. "I'm here to suggest we make a break for it while we can and escape out the back."

"I don't think there is a back."

"So we improvise."

Wiley arched a single eyebrow.

"Let's just go brazen it out and 'exit stage left' via the front door while Sven still has Kit absorbed in darts and weaves."

Wiley did up his jeans, pulled on his light sweater, and plastered himself to the wall. He slid along it and peered past the curtain.

"I'm going on three," Wiley whispered. "One, two…." He lifted a third finger and darted away.

Holt followed.

They tiptoed with complete lack of stealth to the front of the store. Kit didn't deign to turn and look at them. Holt waved at Elaine, winced as the bells on the door chimed, and dashed down the sidewalk to catch up with Wiley.

"We're ridiculous." Wiley laughed and bumped into Holt. "What now?"

"Go walk and then nap in the park? Then find lunch?" Holt said as a million filthy things burst in his imagination.

"Yeah. I like the sound of that." Wiley slid his arm around Holt's waist.

Holt's chest constricted. He covered Wiley's hand with his, tucked Wiley against him, and didn't hurry the several blocks to the park.

"GENTLEMEN, let me see it from the top." Sarah pressed Play and stayed in the corner of the studio.

Holt took him in their frame, held his gaze, nodded the beat, and started them across the floor. Wiley hummed along as they danced. He forgot to mind his concentration point, up and past Holt's shoulder, and Holt was in too close. Wiley's heart floated as light as his feet.

Their footwork didn't stumble, and Holt led them into and around the curves, and didn't get tangled in the final crossover arms flourish and spin.

They stood in silence, and Wiley looked from the smolder in Holt's eyes to the sensuous, wanting lift of Holt's mouth. He looked back up and grinned, and heat flared behind Holt's gaze.

Sarah came to stand a few feet from them, clasped her hands neatly, and smiled. "I believe we are finished."

"Really? We just got here." Holt glanced at Wiley. "That irredeemable?"

"That good. At this stage I feel you leaving with confidence and certainty in the steps is better than overworking it." Sarah shrugged one shoulder. "We could run some drills, put you through your paces, grapevine for fifteen-minute heats."

"Or we agree with your expertise and not overwork it." Holt held out a hand and then did a neat bow over hers when she took it. "Thank you, Miss Sarah. I can honestly say it turned out to be a pleasure."

"It is all mine. At least until the reception and we see how you do," she said with a bit less starch than usual.

"Miss Sarah," Wiley said and shook her hand. "Thank you."

"Thank me by remembering your lift, your carriage, the roll in your feet." She smiled. "Good night, gentlemen. I trust you'll do very well indeed. Until the big day, then—I'm looking forward to it."

"So am I," Wiley said without thinking. He retrieved his things and went to the door, waited for Holt to join him, and they walked to the corner together, as had become their routine.

Wiley readied to ask Holt to come home with him. Their engagement might be fake but what he craved from and with Holt was real, and he was determined to say yes and have it. Even if it came to an end.

Holt held Wiley's gaze and his lips parted. He ran a finger up Wiley's neck.

"Can I walk you home?"

"Yes." A shiver of anticipation racked Wiley.

Holt's arm enveloped him, and Wiley trotted to keep pace.

They got to his house and up the walkway and then onto the porch.

Holt turned and pressed their hips together.

"Do you want to come in?" Wiley asked before Holt could say anything.

"Yes," Holt seemed to grit out.

Wiley dug in his pocket and unlocked the door, and Holt pushed him inside.

"Do you want any lem—" Wiley started to tease.

Holt kicked the door shut, lifted and wrapped Wiley's legs around his waist, and pulled him into a searing kiss.

Holt's flannel shirt, tailored for on-camera wear, split up the back. Wiley laughed and split it the rest of the way, helped Holt get it past Holt's wide wrists, and immediately untucked his T-shirt and tugged it up and over Holt's head.

Holt carried him through the house, one arm slung under his butt, the other feeling along the wall and into the door of Wiley's bedroom as they kissed.

Wiley kicked his shoes away and worked his socks off. He leaned way back and thrilled at Holt's ease in holding him and how Holt watched in appreciation as he stripped from his shirt and sweater in one go. Holt's fingers dug into him, and Holt's teeth scraped over his nipple, and he knotted his hands in Holt's fine hair.

Holt walked to the bed and dropped Wiley onto it, ripped off the rest of his clothes, dealt with Wiley's using the same brutal efficiency, and then landed atop Wiley in purposeful, possessive weight.

Awareness flooded him of how long he'd wanted this. From the moment Holt had called him Coy in the park. How much he wanted it to outlast tonight. He trembled and dug his hands into Holt's shoulders.

Wiley's legs had to spread wide for Holt to fit between them, and the strain from it, the differential, buzzed under his skin.

"I haven't…." Wiley closed his eyes on a moan as Holt rubbed their cocks together. "I haven't done anything in a while."

Holt's rumbly laughter was hot and hungry. "I can't last long enough anyway," he got out between kisses. "Good—so sweet and good." He levered up, grabbed Wiley's hips, and increased the speed and strength of their rutting.

The bed knocked the wall and squeaked the opposite direction as Wiley was forced up the mattress. He dug his heels in, braced a hand on the headboard, and flattened the other on Holt's chest. He couldn't get enough of how hot and hard and powerful Holt was, outmatched him, and moved. How safe it felt like this, how urgently it pitched his desire.

Holt took his hand and slid them down together to fist their cocks. Wiley muttered incoherencies and lost purchase on the bed as his toes curled painfully.

He came and came and unraveled in Holt's arms. Holt slowed to watch him, tugging his cock and thumbing the tip until his nerves were on fire and he was utterly spent. Then Holt grunted and fell forward and staggered his hands so his bulk blotted out everything, so tenderly and right, and used Wiley's willingness to lay there boneless and moaning, fucking the damp crease of Wiley's thigh.

Holt stiffened and a guttural noise sounded from his throat. He dragged himself against Wiley with diminishing speed and then collapsed.

Wiley vibrated with pleasure from every point Holt gently kissed and touched as they rolled onto their sides. He caught Holt's cheeks in his hands and smiled into Holt's mouth as they kissed, and kept smiling as Holt settled onto his chest.

He drew lazy circles on Holt's back, shut his eyes, and listened to Holt fall asleep.

Chapter Eight

HOLT lay, content as he'd ever been. Wiley was pillowed on his arm as he watched Wiley sleep in the early, densely colorful sunrise.

He marveled at how Wiley fit perfectly in the curve of his body. Loved the feel of Wiley under him, completely, as he'd held Wiley's hips and demanded a second, then a third round that Wiley gave so generously. Needed the way he could protect and keep Wiley tucked beside him.

There was nothing to describe his wild desire and near-savage want and satisfaction of having Wiley as he did last night. He hadn't ever been so insatiable and demanding, and then appeased, before. With anyone. Or then woken the morning after, replete and wanting more and more.

He combed Wiley's hair this way and that and drew delicate shapes on Wiley's sleep-warm skin. What if they could stay like this—together, unguarded, nothing fake—well past the episode ending?

The thought didn't shock him. It had built under the surface the past several days. Years. But it was probably unwise.

Wiley snuffled and snuggled closer, and Holt allowed his heart to hope, just a little. They could talk about it, maybe. How amazing they were together, and that had to mean they should find out what staying together longer could bring. To see what Wiley would answer. He had to know.

He ignored the duty to check the time, his phone, in with the world.

This was the only world he wanted for a while. A long, long while.

Eventually he'd get up and make them coffee. Some semblance of breakfast. But he liked that Wiley slept and how relaxing this was, so he kept putting eventually off.

"Morning," he whispered as Wiley finally stirred.

The sun was full up, its color leached to white, and Holt heard the indistinct rumble of traffic in the distance. It occurred to him that tomorrow they would wake—separately—and go get not-married.

"Good morning." Wiley blinked and smiled sleepily, and then seemed to come online. He sat upright.

Holt battled back dread that Wiley would regret this or run from him.

Wiley leaned far down and disappeared past the edge of the mattress. "We're almost late," he said as he grappled up, holding his phone. "You take the guest shower. Carla can feed us."

Wiley threw the covers away, paused, twisted around to give Holt a kiss, and then another. Then he sprang from bed before Holt could catch him for more.

He flopped down and covered his face with Wiley's pillow. Relief made him giddy. Made him want to be late. They could be late—who cared. He could be late for once in his life.

Holt thought about everyone's dedication and the grueling shooting schedule they still had to keep and Kit likely never letting him live it down, and gave in to reality.

The shower heated quickly, and he was clean in under ten minutes.

He emerged prepared to show up on set in yesterday's clothes and smiled at the powder blue XXL CarlaCakes T-shirt and plaid dress shirt still in cellophane on the counter.

Wiley also left him a comb, toothbrush, and toothpaste. He gladly made use of them. The T-shirt fit fine, the dress shirt a bit snug, so he left it unbuttoned, but it worked.

"That's a good look on you," Wiley teased as Holt ventured to the living room. His hair was damp and his neck pink from the shower. "Don't lift your arms over your head, though. Grandma got that shirt for me years ago, even knowing it was huge on me, because it was on very good sale, you see, but you'll pop the seams."

"I'll keep that in mind." Holt noticed the small pile of his things Wiley had collected on the side table. He jammed them into his pockets and gave Wiley a quick kiss. Wiley's eager response emboldened him to say, "We should talk later. I mean, I want to discuss something important."

"Interesting." Wiley kissed Holt's jaw. "But yes, of course. As soon as we're not running late somewhere, we'll talk."

"Good." Holt gathered Wiley to him and tightened his arms. He kissed Wiley again and then had to pull back and rest their foreheads together and pull in a deep breath. Anything more and they'd be really late. "Ready?"

Wiley sighed. "Another day, another layer." But he smiled as he locked up and smiled deeper when Holt caught his hand and held it the short walk to the bakery.

Wiley let go the instant they entered the front door. Holt stared in disbelief at the tables pushed together in the center of the room and seated at them….

"Mom? Dad." Holt turned. "Brent?"

"Wow," Wiley said on a thready breath. "Your parents. Your other brother. This is…. Wow."

This was not how Holt wanted the morning to go. The day. Anything.

Not at all, but especially not after last night and still being able to taste and smell and feel Wiley everywhere.

"Wiley?" he breathed, picking up on Wiley's controlled panic and hard shift. "Please don't." He fumbled for Wiley's hand, but Wiley sidestepped and met his mom halfway as she got up to greet them.

Holt's pulse hammered a warning as Wiley seemed to gather himself, dismiss something, and then visibly move past from what they'd shared last night and woke to, newfound.

"Dad," he managed and shook his father's hand, then moved in for a brief hug. "Surprise."

"We could both say that. Good to see you, Holt."

Clint Leydon was tall and broad and silver where once he'd been light blond. Holt took after him in every way—the eldest of three boys—and most resembled his father, Holt's grandfather. The constant comparisons growing up had always made Holt proud, not annoyed.

Margery Leydon pushed past her husband and enveloped Holt in a hug, an impressive feat for such a petite woman.

"Kit has explained the whole thing," she said into his ear.

Holt momentarily froze. "The whole thing?"

She leaned back and cupped his cheek. "How you reconnected and how it got serious so fast and you with your privacy, and then the need for absolute secrecy." She made a dignified huff. "Why that extended to your family—me—I don't know. But that doesn't mean I'm any less thrilled for you and Wiley."

"Thank you, Mom." As much as disappointment continued to throb in his belly and he was wary as to their being here, he couldn't deny how good it was to see her. Everyone.

Margery was about to say more, but Brent cut in.

"You old dog, or should I say dark horse," Brent said and pulled Holt in for a hug. "She's been practicing what to say to you guys the whole ride here."

"I'll buy you a beer."

"Make it a case." Brent laughed and moved back. "It's fine. She's just nervous."

Kit most resembled their mother. Brent was the brother who looked part of the family when they were together but you wouldn't pick out of a lineup as belonging.

"Where's Lina?"

Brent had married his college girlfriend the year before Kit's show launched. Sometimes he still brought it up to razz how Kit timed it on purpose.

"Work, but she'll be here for the wedding tomorrow. You know she wouldn't miss it."

"Sorry to drag you from your work."

"I think pediatric dentistry will survive the few days I'm not in the trenches." Brent gave Holt another half hug. "It's good to be here."

Holt tried to catch Wiley's eye so he could reintroduce them, but Wiley steadfastly held conversation with Holt's parents.

"Hi, everyone. Good morning. Sorry to interrupt the reunion. I'm Elaine. Director, producer, jack-of-all-trades." She set her binder open on the table. "We're going to film this segment very informally. Rick— that's him." She pointed him out. "He'll be moving and getting close-ups and some person-to-person interactions. Janet is on live content. We don't want the same coverage as we'd get if Rick was streaming, so this can be more private and just-family feeling. Try not to look directly at either of them if you can."

Crew members brought trays of cake slices to the table, and they spent some time with Elaine, arranging it to look haphazard and plentiful but not in a messy way. Carla set finished cakes on the display cases and counters and filled the case trays with brightly frosted cupcakes.

Wiley wouldn't look at him. His parents were here and Brent was here. Filming was going to happen like this was all no big deal, like his whole world hadn't been changed, made perfect, and then ripped from him.

As Holt watched, his wariness became disquiet, and that blossomed into anger.

"That's about it." Elaine checked the time. "As you taste, talk about the cake and what you like and don't like without being too critical, and otherwise converse naturally. It's fine if there's some silences but chatty—overlapping chatter too—is ideal. Once we're done here, Kit will do some solo with you all in the background, and then he and Carla will be in the kitchen for the flavors and decoration reveal. Good?"

Holt said through his teeth, "A moment." He stopped from saying more and tugged Kit into a corner to talk. This was the angriest he'd been at Kit in years, and he didn't want to upset anyone.

Other than Kit.

He needed a full minute before he could speak. "So we're just going to lie to Mom and Dad and Brent?"

"Our parents watch the show and check the internet and have friends who send nosy messages. It's not like they didn't know you are fake-marrying Wiley," Kit hissed.

Holt narrowed his eyes. "That doesn't mean you had to drag them into it."

"They descended last night, intent on a reunion and some catch-up time with Wiley and the old haunts about town. What would you have me do, put them on a tour bus of local birding hotspots until the reception?"

"Yes, that's exactly what I'd have you do. Something."

"Something is being done and will be done. They'll be taken care of, and besides, having them here doing this gives us more control than if I cut them loose to wander."

"Here in an ambush and making Wiley squirm." Holt's temper flared. Wiley still hid from him, and that's what drove his anger. "You could have warned me, at least."

Kit drew back and his expression turned speculative. "Where is your phone?"

Holt pulled it from his pocket and glared.

"Unlock it. Please."

Holt almost didn't, but they were under scrutiny from quite the audience, and he didn't want to play at this much longer.

Kit tapped away, exhaled, and held up a hand. "Don't tell me what had you so… distracted. That's not my business. But I tried to warn you. I even called." He gave the phone back. "There. I took it off silent and turned your notifications back on. Now I'm going to go tell Mom the strawberry chiffon is my favorite cake flavor, because it's definitely hers, and—Holt? For what it's worth, I'm sorry."

Holt checked his phone. "Oh shit," he breathed, and his anger dissipated into regret.

Fifteen messages, two emails, and one missed call, all from Kit.

He sent a text to Kit. *No, I'm sorry.*

Kit looked up from talking to Mom and waved. Forgiven that easily, because what made Kit infuriating also made him pretty amazing.

Next, Holt texted Wiley. *For reference*, he wrote, stared at it and thought how cold and formal and then sent it anyway, followed by forwarding all of Kit's emails and copied messages.

He returned to his seat and watched Wiley scroll and read them, but Wiley didn't otherwise react.

"All right, we are starting filming in five." Elaine counted down, dropped the slate, and for a moment there was awkward silence, but then Kit asked Brent to pass the banana pudding cake and how was his trip in.

"Everything as it should be?" Clint asked quietly.

"Yeah, Kit and I sometimes butt heads on the best way to capture a segment. I didn't realize how much we butted heads over until it was my wedding."

"And you wouldn't have it any other way."

"I suppose not." Holt sighed. "That and you know I hate surprises."

Clint chuckled. "And I wouldn't have it any other way."

Holt grumped. "Try the vanilla bean cake, Dad."

"The vanilla bean is delicious. I experimented and paired it with a bite of candied ginger, and that was amazing." Margery held out her hand. "Brent, pass the candied ginger again, please." She gave it to Clint. "What's your favorite, Wiley?"

"Coconut-cherry," Holt answered automatically. He held up his hands. "Sorry."

"It is coconut-cherry."

Margery *tsk*ed sadly. "What a shame that Holt hates coconut."

"I know. I almost left him over it."

Brent snickered, but Margery took it in stride without showing even a small crack.

"He has the good sense to like chocolate, at least," she said. "But then Holt always wanted cookies or pastries far more than cake."

"Maybe we should have a wedding cookie tower," Wiley mused. "Carla? What do you think?"

"Sorry, I can't hear you over my delicious cake."

Wiley shrugged. "Well, I tried." He fiddled with his fork. "I wanted to make sure I told you thank you for the cards."

"Cards?" The plural caught Holt's attention.

"Oh, nothing over and above. Christmas, that sort of thing. And of course, you know I've been glad to." Margery speared a hunk of almond-and-mocha cake. "Everything you bake is incredible, Carla. I think we'll need something with seven tiers."

Carla beamed with pride and gave Margery a different plate. "This one's citrus drizzle."

"Citrus drizzle? I'm doomed." Margery nudged the cake toward Clint. "Honey, you eat some first, because I'm definitely finishing the rest. And that bite you take is crucial because it will give me room for the rest of the strawberry chiffon."

"I appreciated them. Over and above." Wiley fiddled with the tag on his teabag. "It meant a lot to me you reached out after Grandma died, and then holidays after."

Margery set down her fork and turned to Wiley. "I know, dear. And thank you for your sweet little drawings in return. I've kept them in a book."

"That's so nice. And I like sending them to an appreciative audience." Wiley's pensiveness cleared as he smiled. "A card a year isn't exactly pen pals," he said to Brent. "But you know your mom."

Brent nodded fondly. "I do."

Holt watched the interplay almost agape. He supposed outside of this, he'd never have found out unless by some chance he came across something from Wiley at his parents' house. That made him ache.

"To think, so much of that time you were dating Holt in secret. I never got the tiniest sense of it, and I'm usually pretty good at that sort of thing." Margery laughed. "But then you were always good at quietly observing or even hiding. It's what made you such a good foil to Kit." She combed Wiley's hair back. "But you're a perfect fit for Holt."

Wiley blushed and Holt tore his gaze away. He got up and went to the kitchen for coffee.

Horny to shocked to angry to tender to horny again—talk about whiplash.

"Everything okay?" Wiley came into the kitchen and started the coffee Holt hadn't gotten around to making.

"Nearly. Yes." Holt shut his eyes. "We walked into the bakery and a whole, whole lot more than I was ready for."

"You can say that again." Wiley puttered and although he seemed relaxed, he kept a certain distance from Holt. "Thank you for the texts and stuff. From Kit. I discovered I had emails—that I hadn't read—when you forwarded yours."

"Yeah. Muting my phone… maybe not the wisest move."

"Maybe none of that was, but it's cleared up and we can move on." Wiley pulled the coffeepot from the maker, and a last few drips sizzled on the element.

Holt registered that and caught Wiley behind the display cases. "Move on?"

"Yeah. No reason for regrets or angst but no reason to declare what isn't there." Wiley shrugged casually. "We enjoyed it, won't dwell on it, and have to deal with the fact that your family is here eating cake. That kind of move on."

"And then?"

"Not get married, like we promised." Wiley smiled.

Holt recognized Wiley's on-camera smile. Seeing it—Wiley actually using it on him—twisted his heart. He wanted to argue, to point out his angst from having zero regret other than if Wiley slipped away from him, but what was there to say? If all Wiley wanted was to move on, he had to move on.

"Right. Like we promised." Holt glanced into the bakery front and caught Kit waving both hands in laughter at their parents. He snuffed his earlier hope and sealed the crack in his heart. "A lot of people are counting on it."

"Exactly."

Holt sighed, let Wiley get ahead of him, and then followed.

"Try this one," Margery said as he approached. "Chocolate, chocolate, and chocolate. Or as I called it, heavenly."

Holt had a modest bite and pitched his voice low. "I am sorry you found out like you did. Wiley and I…." He wasn't certain what to say that wouldn't make her worry. "It all went so much faster than I could keep up with."

"Which, maybe it's better that way." Margery leaned close. "Your father and I endured a year and a half engagement with his parents and my parents bickering over every detail and wound up with the wedding of his mother's dreams. It was hardly our wedding in the end. We just showed up to her show."

Holt laughed. If only she knew. "Still, I can't imagine why I didn't think to tell you."

Margery glanced at Wiley and back to Holt. "Oh, sweetheart. I can." Her quick smile faded. "I'll admit it was a jolt at first. Even a little bruise. But Kit called and explained, and you know his way of making things make sense."

"Don't I ever. And Dad?"

"He's fine. He's long assumed you'd come home married with a couple of kids before you decided to tell us." She waved a hand. "Besides, he's always liked Wiley. Me too."

"Me three." Holt stared as Wiley bantered with Brent and Kit. Had he imagined this, over the years? Returning to Odalia and getting to know Wiley as more than his kid brother's friend but a great person—an enticing, attractive person he'd never fully allowed himself to want? Holt's jaw tightened with the sure answer. "I like him a whole lot."

"I know, and I'm so glad." Margery straightened and nabbed the strawberry chiffon. "Let's return to the important business of cake and deciding our top three so your brother can ignore it and order the cake he's had planned all along."

Holt spent the rest of the morning trying to catch Wiley's eye or get him alone, but Wiley proved elusive. He put coconut-cherry as his number one flavor on the card Carla handed out and stared at it until his mom tugged it from his hand.

"You're almost there and Wiley is almost all yours." She squeezed his arm. "You'll make it."

"I hope so." He smiled for her and ignored the dark and doubt trying to take hold in his heart.

WILEY blinked at the ceiling from the daybed in his office because he couldn't stand to lie in his bed. Getting back home and picking up their discarded clothes he hadn't had time to deal with the previous morning—when he'd also thought he'd had all the time in the world—was bad enough.

Trying to sleep where he and Holt had just been together, in a bed still thick with their scent? Impossible.

He imagined Miss Sarah would be disappointed with his efforts to get rest. He flopped onto his side to change the view and wished they'd had a lesson tonight. Something to help him get over how his heart had maybe quietly broken over cake and small talk as his mind caught up to the full ramifications of what they'd done and couldn't have and demanded he see reason.

Talking to Holt's family had been nice. In a vacuum. The full force of being with the kind people who were your soon-to-be not-in-laws was far less nice.

He was relieved their surprise arrival was a huge cluster that Kit had worked to contain and not purposeful.

But that didn't make spending the day with them and Holt and keeping his smile up and his distance held any easier.

It didn't get him any closer to knowing how to end this. Or how Holt wanted to talk to him about something important and he'd done everything possible to avoid that, even as he was desperate to know what it was.

His phone buzzed, so loud in the quiet room it startled a yelp from him.

"Carla?"

"Wiley, I'm sorry to wake you up, but—"

"I'm awake. I've been awake." Carla sounded edgy and like she was in a cave. "Where are you?"

"The staging shed. Don't imagine the very, very worst, but you should get over here. Now."

"On my way."

He flew through getting dressed and together and out the door. Wiley mostly walked, so he kept his car in the garage, and the minutes that added to getting away seemed to take forever.

Wiley drove way over the speed limit, but it was four in the morning and no one was out. Way over the speed limit was as slow as he could endure going, anyway. He kept his eyes peeled for the landmarks that meant he was close to the out-of-business self-storage lot where production rented a huge hangar to warehouse everything gathered and needed for the wedding.

Good thing. He might not have remembered how to get there otherwise.

He pulled in and parked behind Carla—the only other car—and ran to the side entrance where a light was on.

"Carla?" Wiley burst through the door and knew immediately why she called in such a state. He hadn't been here before to know an exact configuration of waiting boxes and bins, but it didn't matter. There were no waiting boxes and bins, only disarray. He couldn't quite believe what he was seeing. "Are you hurt? Did you get mugged?"

"I got here and found it like this." Carla patted a plastic bin set on an otherwise empty table. "I woke up in this cold sweat, realizing I forgot to add rose-gold nonpareils to the fondant tufts on one layer and figured I'd just come over and do it. I have the keycode for the door, and this isn't early for me, you know. And. Well."

Wiley scanned the wreckage for any sign of the cake. "Is it gone?"

"Yeah. I didn't find hunks of it anywhere, so I guess whoever did this carted it off with everything else. Even your suits. Who takes suits?"

"Carla, your cake. No. The whole reason to be in this mess. The only reason you're here at four in the morning to tuft fondant. For a fake wedding." A fluorescent bulb hummed incessantly, and he shivered. "It's cold in here."

She nodded. "To preserve the cake and flowers. Those are gone too."

"Who takes cake and flowers?"

"And candles and linens and the ugly stick silverware. And Wiley," Carla said miserably, "your village. I looked all over but couldn't find it."

Wiley blinked rapidly and cried anyway.

"Oh, oh, honey. I'm sorry." Carla pulled him into a hug. "There's been robberies in town, and Chief Wilkins had a talk with downtown business owners to be on alert, but I never thought about anything like this happening." She squeezed tighter. "We can figure this out. We have so far."

He shook his head against her hair. "I love him," he whispered. The confession escaped on its own.

"Oh, oh. Oh, Wiley." Carla pulled away and took hold of his arms. "I thought so. From almost the start, but I didn't want to say anything unless you got all stubborn about denying, like you do." She frowned, and sympathetic tears shone in her eyes. "We can figure that out too. If you want."

"I don't know if he wants," Wiley said miserably. "He definitely *wanted* me, and that was incredible…." He blushed as he admitted it, and Carla's arch look registered as he batted back her rising questions. "Yes, fine, whatever. And the morning after was amazing, and it gave me ideas I never should have had."

"Ideas?"

"Suffice to say I wanted to maybe get married for real."

"I knew it," she exclaimed. "Sorry, just…. Called it."

"Points to you, then. And I also thought it could be possible Holt did too." Wiley remembered the warmth in his belly that whole morning, from waking together and it feeling right, to getting ready in sync with Holt, through walking hand in hand to the bakery. "But then suddenly we were at the bakery and his whole family and the camera crew were there, and it totally threw me. Then when I said hey, no regrets, but let's not dwell on it and move on, he agreed." He felt himself pout.

Carla groaned. "Of course he agreed, you lout. What else was he supposed to do? Hustle you behind the pantry racks and have a huge heart-to-heart to hash out the details of probably being in love with you back, with his whole family and the camera crew there? Have you seen how he looks at you? I have. Same way you look at him when you think no one sees."

In love with you back zinged around Wiley's chest.

"Holt wanted to talk to me about something important. That's what he said that morning. I thought it was going to be good, but then, the bakery. And things snowballed and now we're here." He grimaced when Carla punched him. "Ow! What's that for?"

"You earned it. The big hunk you're in love with wants to make serious talk after an amazing night together and you get in your own way and decide business as usual, then? Of course, he could have come after you and insisted and explained, but of course he didn't because he's stoic and only wants to fix things, not cause damage." Carla huffed. She pursed her lips and glanced around. "Wow, well. That's too much to sort out all at once. But we will. So, let's deal with each of the steps for dealing with this and then go from there."

Wiley's mind raced. "Have you called anyone else yet?"

"No."

"That fancy boutique mall you like so much and I rarely let you drag me to is not even an hour away, right? South on the highway?"

Carla frowned. "Yes. But what does that have to do with working this to for-real marry Holt?"

"I don't know." They connected in Wiley's mind, but he couldn't explain it. "But I do know that's a start, and I have to do something."

"Or… you could find Holt and have that talk?"

"Nope," he said before he really thought it. He had to do the fixing, and fix this first.

She sighed. "I like you two together. I always have. Even when we were dorks and he didn't much notice us, he was always far kinder and cooler to us than Kit ever was. And I'll do whatever I can to help you make it work. But Wiley, after being in Odalia this long and saying yes to all this—" Carla gestured to the mess around them. "—don't you dare run now."

"I'm not running. I promise. Thank you." Wiley kissed her cheek and then walked toward the door. He patted his pockets by rote and noted his keys, wallet, phone as adrenaline surged through him. "Okay. You stay here and call the police. And Elaine. She's probably best to start coping with all this. I'll be back."

"Back from where?"

"Doing whatever I can."

"Wiley," Carla called. He stopped, and she huffed but waved him on. "Good luck."

Chapter Nine

HOLT paced without cease.

The mansion swarmed with activity as everyone pitched in to try to rescue the apparent ruin of the wedding. Everyone except Holt, who found he could do nothing but check his phone, pace, grab someone and ask if there'd been any updates, pace, and check his phone again.

Everyone stayed out of his way.

He'd given a brief statement to the police, who had come to interview everyone. He'd tried and failed to help Ben arrange seating for the ceremony. His father had talked him down from going in search of Wiley, making the infuriatingly good point that Wiley would know to come here, but Holt had no sure idea where to look for Wiley.

So he paced.

For efficiency he had started pacing a circuit. He passed through the mansion, onto the porch, along the front, onto the other porch, and back inside. He avoided the oval patio.

He counted seven circuits and paused at the room meant for him to get dressed and ready for his not-wedding that was still barreling toward happening, and tried to pull a plan together from the scatter in his mind.

"Here you are."

Holt whirled around and nearly doubled over in relief. "Wiley." He shook his head. "Here I am? Of course I'm here. Where have you been? Carla said something about a boutique, and you've been gone hours and not answering your phone. Are you all right? She said you weren't hurt but are you hurt?"

Wiley was pale but grimly determined and holding so many bulging paper shopping bags the handles of several slinked up his arms like bracelets.

"What is all this?" Holt stepped forward to grab the bags, throw them, and drag Wiley to him.

He stopped and clenched his fists when Wiley stepped back.

"There's more in my car. We should get all this out and make sure it'll do. I couldn't get anything exact, but I think it'll work. It'll be good enough."

"Good enough for what?" Holt rubbed his temple. "Wiley, don't make me stand here asking endless questions. Why didn't you answer my texts or talk to me? What is this?"

"Flower arrangements. Placemats and chargers. Centerpieces—no village buildings, those aren't upscale enough to find at trendy boutiques." Wiley's mouth quivered. "I didn't get plates. Carla has plates. Chef Pete has to have plates."

"What do I care about goddamn plates?" Holt roared.

Wiley rose to his full height and nodded once. "Well. Someone might."

He opened his hands and dropped the bags in a quick succession of dull whacks. One snagged at his wrist and he unceremoniously ripped it free, tossed it on the rest, and then turned on his heel and walked resolutely away without looking back.

"Wiley," Holt called and started after him but tripped on the pile of bags.

He growled and kicked the pile. Twice. Then he started to see what Wiley had gotten.

Nothing matched the notebook clippings or paint chips or plan. No pale colors, no pearl sheen, no fucking rose gold. Textured fabric in colors warm and earthy, hand-turned wood, rustic bouquets of wildflowers. Holt dug in a bag, and out tumbled several ceramic bowls. Down in one stood two goats, and in another, a fat pig.

He buried his head in his hands and groaned.

Then something occurred to him, breaking over his gloom and confusion like sunlight. He jack-knifed to stand and tore from the room.

"Wiley?" He careened through the mansion.

Elaine and then Janet and then Ben pointed. Front, outside, down the lawn.

Holt launched from the porch and ran.

Wiley hadn't even gotten that far, but Holt felt every jarring step.

"Wait," he called and sprinted the final distance. He only caught his breath because Wiley came to a stop. "Kit would hate everything."

Wiley tensed and then his shoulders fell, but he didn't turn around.

"I looked in the bags. I get it, but I don't." Holt inched closer to and then around Wiley. He said what he hadn't been able to stop thinking and hated more than anything. "That could have been it, you know—our exit."

Wiley looked at him at that.

Holt nodded. "And who could blame us if we postponed our dream wedding after everything got ransacked and ruined?"

He watched Wiley's eyes widen in realization and hoped Wiley had thought only to save the wedding for the same reason he'd paced, unable to concentrate on doing anything about it with Wiley gone.

"Even if production could scrounge up replacements, we could say the upset was too much, that it felt wrong to go ahead, any number of things. It's a sympathetic story. People would understand."

Holt hooked a finger under Wiley's chin. "Coy." His voice cracked and he swallowed. "Please tell me."

"And we needed that exit more than replacement anything, didn't we? Why replace what you're not—" Wiley huffed a short laugh. "I didn't even think about that. All I could think about was fixing it. For Carla and her cake—they even stole her cake. And your family. The show, well, the crew. And even Kit."

Holt let Wiley ramble, but it wasn't the answer he longed for.

Wiley went quiet for a bit and then asked, "What did you do?"

"Do? When?"

"While I was gone. Build some benches? Toss together a rose-covered trellis? Make Kit a fainting couch?"

"Wished you back here with me."

Wiley frowned. "That's it?"

"That's all I could manage."

Wiley let out a low, soft breath. "Is it still a good story if we bravely go forth and not cancel?"

"Motivation?" Holt's heart skipped a beat.

"Can-do spirit. Save the show." Wiley stared into Holt's eyes. "Because all I could think about was how desperately I wanted to marry you."

"And why would that be?"

Wiley smiled. "I love you."

Holt closed his eyes and fought to breathe. He easily found Wiley's lips with his and pulled them into a tight embrace. He kissed Wiley's ear and eyebrow and dimple and chin, went up the other side, and drew reluctantly back.

"I love you. So much." Holt traced the curve of moles on Wiley's cheek and thrilled at the heat of Wiley's blush under his touch. "I think that would probably be the best story ever told."

"Okay, good. Let's do that, then." Wiley leaned back. "So we're clear, I don't care about plates either. Or the wedding."

"Not the wedding?"

"Just the marriage."

Holt had to kiss Wiley again. Hard. "Then let's get married."

WILEY let Kit fuss with his bow tie and pocket square and smiled as Holt walked into the room.

"It's too late for you not to see each other, but you know you're not supposed to see each other." Kit gave a final primp and moved to admire his work. "You'll do. It is a very good thing this shifted to plucky and sincere in the face of adversity, because the fashion and everything else that shifted—not my standard."

Holt held out his arms and surveyed his outfit. "Maybe not, but I'm comfortable."

"Of course you are, Holty dear, you're in your own terrible clothes." Kit adjusted Holt's tie. "It's good you had something resembling a suit. I was about to make you wear Dad's."

"I'm surprised that's up to your standards."

"Well, no. But at least it matches." Kit got the boutonnieres he'd made from the wildflowers Wiley bought and pinned them on.

"I still say you should let me wear my tool belt."

Kit rolled his eyes. Any quip he had in return got lost in rising commotion outside. "Police again, maybe? Ooh, perhaps the robbers brought everything back." He hurried from the room and down the hall.

Wiley looked to Holt, who shrugged and caught his hand as he passed to follow.

The mansion had emptied of crew and early invited guests. They were all clustered on the porch watching a veritable parade start up the driveway.

"Whatever is this?" Kit went down the stairs to the lawn and the group assembling there.

Wiley recognized the mom and daughters from the bakery the other morning. "Holt, we kind of know them."

She saw him pointing her out and elbowed her daughters and waved. They each had a vase of flowers or a vase without flowers or flowers without a vase. As did the rest of the group.

Kit gestured Wiley and Holt over. As they neared, Elaine and company arrived with folding tables and a notepad.

Elaine held up a pen. "Everyone, if you'd like, please sign here and we'll be sure and thank you on social and figure out something more. And stick around, because we're putting together a lunch garden party—Chef Cortez is bringing his food truck!"

The fans cheered as Elaine marshaled the group into a line, and as the line passed, fans took selfies with Kit and went to pose on the porch with the crew and then set off to wander the grounds. As the table filled with flowers and vases bought at the pop-up store, Wiley noticed a growing random assortment of village figurines.

"Please tell me you're getting this," Kit murmured at Janet between selfies.

She gave the thumbs-up and kept filming.

"I don't like the price paid. My beautiful plans and layers, gone." Kit eyed Holt and Wiley's suits with disdain. "But if I'd have known the buzz and drama some bumbling real-life criminals would bring to the proceedings, I'd have planned it myself."

"Yes. With arrangements for acceptable backups just-so-happened to be tucked away in your B and B room or something to save the day. What a missed opportunity," Wiley said, wry but light enough to tease, and smiled at Kit's put-upon sigh.

He and Holt stayed until the last fan donated her vase.

After that, they were firmly but politely scooted out of the way, and he watched as Kit and the crew descended and tried to make sense from the mishmash of his frantic purchases, mansion pieces, the slightly battered but still blowsy flowers, and odds and ends sent by various stores and friends and fans.

Pete had brought plates. Along with every baked goodie Carla had in the store.

Carla tracked them down.

"Wiley. *You* figured it out. I'm proud and happy and weepy and on the verge of destroying this incredible makeup. How dare you." She pulled him into a tight hug. "Best, craziest *yes* ever said, in the history of yes-saying. I think after this one you can quit and go back to careful nos."

"I might. Not." He pushed back so he could get a look at her. "But hey. Good thing you pestered me—again and again and again and again—after all."

"I'm looking forward to our next adventure being remarkably staid." She dabbed at the threat of tears but grinned.

Wiley tugged her close again. "Thank you."

"Congrats, Wiley. I'm so happy for you," she whispered. She hugged Holt next. "And? Starting after your honeymoon, you have to come in more than mornings, because there's so many online orders, we'll be baking around the clock for months."

"Ever thought of hiring someone and teaching them the ropes?" Wiley shrugged. "I am happy for you, and the bakery, but I'm not doing more than mornings or Sundays." He looked at Holt and back to Carla. "I'm kinda making plans for other things."

"Valid. And maybe the best no you've ever said. Also, yay." Carla hummed. "Hire an apprentice baker. I like that." She held up a finger, went to grab a bakery box, and handed it to Wiley.

"I kept it separate so it didn't get damaged in the transfer. Unforeseen quality move."

Their cake topper—the coconut-cherry top tier of their actual cake—stood on an alternating stack of danishes and bear claws.

Holt pinched a bite of danish. "Awesome. Thank you."

"They both freeze great, so you can have one of each on your first anniversary." Carla checked her phone. "Yeah, I gotta go figure out how to display and serve everything from croutons to cupcakes." She kissed Wiley's cheek and then Holt's. "Save a dance for me. Both of you."

Holt eased the topper from the stack and wrapped a danish and a bear claw in a tissue sheet, tucked them in the box, and bit through one of the others.

"I was just standing here thinking we'd missed lunch."

Wiley took a hunk of bear claw. "And breakfast."

Holt stopped chewing and smiled as he watched Wiley.

"What?"

"It's hard to explain."

"Try." Wiley wiped icing from his chin. "Please."

Holt leaned in to lick the spot and kept hold of Wiley. "I always liked coming to GB's house and doing work and talking with you. Even as a kid you were smart and funny and seemed to think I was the same. I never thought of you as anything but Kit's friend, but also as the best of Kit's choices in friends." His gaze fell to Wiley's hands on his chest. "I went away to college and got on with life, but whenever I visited, there you were. Still smart and funny, but you'd also grown up to be cute as heck, and I couldn't shake how adorable you were and how Kit didn't deserve you."

"Ugh, you creep," Wiley said, but he couldn't stop grinning.

"It wasn't like that," Holt protested.

"I know." Wiley patted him. "You stayed with me when you left too. Lingered on the edges, and then I moved back here and there were so many reminders in the house. You were always kind and helpful and talked to me like I was a real person. Which, nice. And I had the worst crush on Kit. I'm sure you realized that."

"I might have had an inkling," he underplayed. "I'm not sure Kit ever realized." Holt shrugged. "He's like that."

"Ugh, too real. But it's long, long gone. After you left, but before he hightailed it to Hollywood. You know, I thought I wanted to see him again. That's mostly why Carla and I went to the announcement." Wiley realized something as he was saying it. "But one look at you and I basically forgot about him."

Holt growled something and dragged Wiley into a long, demanding, sharing kiss. It told Wiley everything Holt had said would be hard to explain.

"You were a vague, fond memory when I thought about Odalia. But then on announcement day I had one look at you—grown, gorgeous, smarter and funnier you—and I slowly admitted I'd put you out of my mind on purpose."

"Whoa. Really?" That almost winded Wiley. "Is that why you agreed to fake marry me?"

"No. It didn't all occur to me at once. I just knew I had to protect you from Kit's machinations, but it was more than that. It was easy to agree and keep up the pretense and very much not think of any way out because it felt good and right being with you, at your house. That was like coming home. And…." Holt grabbed them another pastry. "It made me think how glad I am that I get to have breakfast for dinner with you every day."

"Let's redo the kitchen."

"Okay."

Wiley laughed. "Sorry, total non sequitur except in my brain, where I was imagining getting dusty and paint-spattered and learning how to grout so I could wind up with a huge double bench we'll both fit on overlooking the backyard and ivy while we eat."

"I like that idea."

"I like you. And what you told me." Wiley kissed Holt. "Thank you for telling me. And for wanting to protect me and falling in love with me almost as much as I fell in love with you in the process."

"I believe we're even," Holt whispered, and kissed Wiley into delirious silence.

They gave in, eventually, to parting so they could finish the show. Wiley stood with Holt in the darkened conservatory that led to the get-married porch. Considering he'd had zero sleep and tons of stress and a marathon sprint, he was remarkably serene.

"Remember how I said the days felt like years?"

Holt squeezed Wiley's hand. "That's because they did."

"Well, today has felt like a minute. At the most."

"Thank goodness we have eternity afterwards." Holt kissed Wiley. "Remember how I said I love you and will you marry me?"

Wiley bit his lip and smiled hugely anyway. "I might."

"Marry me?"

"Love you." Wiley's whole being sang when Holt grumped and dragged him close, surrounding him entirely in his kiss and embrace.

They didn't jump apart when light flooded the room, but Holt did raise his head and scowl.

Kit and the camera crew walked toward them, Kit midsentence. "…and it's pep talk time with my couple. Usually I let you all in on that because that is the true final toss of glitter on all my gorgeous layers, but not this episode." He shooed at the camera. "Don't despair, the real show is about to start, but I want a special moment with my wonderful brother and best friend. Off you go!"

Kit blew a kiss as Rick walked back and then cut away.

"A special moment?" Holt fiddled with his tie. "Make it brief. Please."

"The sincerity, the kinship, the charm. But seriously, his anxiousness is adorable," Kit said, more to Wiley. He cleared his throat. "You two are about to get married—for-real married—and once you walk down that aisle it will all be a glorious blur, so I wanted to tell you how well you've done and I'm so proud and that we really have, out of such an inglorious beginning, pulled together the best episode of this show." He pressed his fingertips under his eyes and inhaled-exhaled deeply. "You may thank me now."

Holt's lips flattened. "Do not tell me you're going to take credit for this."

"Why I most certainly am." Kit nodded knowingly and waved a finger around. "When Wiley started asserting himself with interest on details and choices and you checked out and let it happen, I knew for sure. I had an inkling from almost the very start, and some *oh yes they're goners* antenna twitches, but that?" He snapped his fingers. "Cinched it."

"Cinched what, exactly?" Wiley had more than an inkling but wanted to hear it.

"My dears, my doves. I know people in love when I see them—it's kind of my spectacular expertise. Same as I know we've married more than one couple over the years who aren't." Kit patted their cheeks. "And you two? Tip the scales for the most incredibly in love as I've ever had the pleasure to plan a wedding for, and it's been as plain as the noses on your oblivious faces. So thank the goddess I got you all the way to here—and oh, my stars, what a gauntlet that proved to be—before one of you could mess it all up."

Wiley knew the best thing to do. He didn't mind it a bit.

"Thank you, Kit." He leaned forward from Holt enough to give Kit a hug. "It's been good to reconnect. I mean that, and not only because I got this guy in the process."

"Samesies. You're the only person I'd trust with my Holty." Kit's voice quavered, and he stood and fluffed Wiley's suit jacket. "And you." He hugged Holt. "Are going to take such good care of my bestie. You better continue to deserve him, and I promise I'll visit, but we will not do holidays, only because you know I travel for me-time over those, and okay, enough before I ruin my subtle yet killer smoky eye." He stepped away and tugged his shimmering rose-gold blazer back to perfection.

"I got you this as a wedding gift." Kit pulled a long flat envelope from his breast pocket. "It's the least I could do, since you gave me our highest-rated show and the likely launch of my next one."

"Already?" Holt asked as he took the envelope.

"Let's just say I've had some ideas percolating for a while, and that everyone at the network is very, very happy."

Wiley watched Holt's reaction as he unfolded the crisp, thick packet of letterhead paper. There was amazement and a flicker of annoyance and then a faraway I-got-plans look.

"Kit?" Holt said, elongating the syllable.

"It's nothing. Wait, no, it's a nightmare and a headache. A decades-long headache."

"A headache I can't wait to get started on. Thank you."

"You'll owe so much in taxes and repairs, you'll be cursing my generosity in no time." Kit sounded dry, but his eyes sparkled with delight.

Holt passed the papers to Wiley. The deed to Sinclair Hardware in Holt's and Wiley's names. Wiley was genuinely surprised. Kit had a knack for grand gestures, but they weren't usually as thoughtful and lasting and expensive as this.

"When I called the town council about interest in funding a restoration for the building or even buying it, they said it was under confidential contract." Holt shook his head. "You bring me in there, you give me ideas, then you buy it out from under me. You're so sneaky. Always. You've always been so sneaky."

"And thank goodness I am." Kit tucked the deed in the envelope and back into his pocket. "I'll keep it safe until later, as you two are going to be quite otherwise occupied. Wiley, I also got you a whole new drafting table setup and markers and such that my adorable art store expert said were a must, but they don't fit in my pocket. We'll talk about that later too."

"What later?"

"Your storied design and comic or whatever career, obviously." Kit pulled in a long breath and held it. "Now. Time for the final act. Good?"

"Perfect," Wiley said, and Holt tightened his hand.

Kit nodded, did a few voice exercises, and disappeared out the door onto the porch. "Who's ready to *Marry Me*?" reverberated over the sound system and the guests cheered.

"How does he do that? I feel suddenly indebted to him for life."

"All part of his magic, I guess." Holt leaned back. "Hey, I just realized you still haven't picked a big trip destination yet. For our honeymoon. Where do you want to go?"

"Camping," Wiley said without hesitation.

"On the coast."

"Definitely on the coast. With mountains nearby."

"I think that can be arranged." Holt turned and took hold of Wiley's other hand, beautiful and tall and everything in his plaid shirt, dressy work pants, and corduroy blazer. "Are you ready to marry me?"

Wiley grinned. "Yes."

"LADIES and gentlemen, I present our newlyweds, Mr. Wiley Grey and Mr. Holt Leydon."

Holt kissed Wiley before they stepped onto the larger porch chosen for the reception from the relative quiet of the connecting room. He kissed Wiley after they came to a halt on the porch three steps later.

"Ahem, happy couple? This way. Everyone, if you could please allow them passage, thank you." Kit waved them toward the large oval patio. "In case anyone doesn't know, I was a rather mischievous little brother and best friend and assigned them to learn and perform a dance at the reception. And here we are. A reception made by each of you, and our amazing fans, and dear Odalia. If it's wonderful, all credit to Miss Sarah, their teacher, and Wiley, the apt pupil. If they're slightly less than wonderful...." He paused dramatically. "It won't happen. They're going to be wonderful."

Kit winked, looped the mic cord, and gave them the floor.

"I'm more nervous about this than when I asked you to marry me in front of everyone at that gazebo. And when we agreed to fake it. And when I realized it wasn't fake. And when we walked down the aisle. And when I said I do." Holt tried to control his breathing.

Wiley laughed indulgently. "Catch me and I'll kiss you."

Holt's nerves went up in smoke. He growled and started forward. Wiley caught him in an approximation of the frame, their song began to play, and Wiley stayed an arm's reach and a step ahead of him the entire dance.

"This is when I knew. That I loved you. It was happening anyway, but having the dance studio to ourselves, holding you in my arms, walking you to the corner in the dark, this music I couldn't get out of my head. Sealed the deal and you into my heart." Holt drew Wiley's hand to his heart's thunder. He wasn't supposed to, but the song was almost over and he didn't care. "Never, ever tell Kit."

"On pain of his being even more insufferable than he already is, because, same."

Holt laughed and stared at Wiley's laughing mouth.

Wiley might have missed a step on purpose.

Holt might have stepped on Wiley's foot.

Whatever happened, Holt managed to catch Wiley as the song ended and kissed him until cheers and catcalls finally penetrated his awareness and made him let go.

They stood at the center of the oval with Wiley tucked against his side as Kit brought him the microphone.

"Yeah, I don't…," he said under his breath, but Kit ignored him and sailed away again.

Wiley squeezed the hand he had at Wiley's hip, and he gave in.

"Well, you can thank Miss Sarah for that. She was incredibly patient while shaping me into an almost not-terrible dancer." He nodded in her direction and waited through a smattering of applause. He tried to keep his tone light, but emotion tugged at it. "I'm not one for speeches, so this mic is going right back to Kit, but marrying Wiley means everything to me, so you being here to share it means everything to us."

The guests laughed and *awww*ed.

"This morning when we discovered the robbery, I was a mess trying to rescue a bigger mess." Holt shook his head at the continuing laughter. "Believe me. I know I'm cool and composed and Mr. Fix-it on the show but, definite mess."

Wiley nodded, which prompted even more laughter and *awww*s.

"And then somewhere in that mess and Wiley and I agreeing we could get married without any fanfare and trying to talk Kit into it, the town and fans and all of you came together as my fix-it." Holt smiled. "So. Kit helped us plan the wedding of our dreams, that got wrecked beyond my repair, and in the end, it turned into the wedding of our life."

Everyone started applauding again, so Holt finished with "Thanks, everybody. Please, enjoy yourselves tonight. I know we will. Now go eat one of Carla's amazing danishes and wash it down with Pete's signature sangria."

He turned off the mic and exhaled. "I think that wasn't the worst."

"I think it was the greatest ever. Dance included." Wiley smiled. "You did it."

"We did it."

"We're married. For real." Wiley's eyes glittered with happiness and desire when he smiled.

Holt set the mic on a table and led Wiley away from the party to the darkened end of the patio. "We are." He kissed Wiley and reveled in them being married, for real, and that Wiley was his forever, no faking.

Kit's voice floated to them. "As soon as the couple can tear themselves away from each other, they're going to mingle. In the meantime, finish off those hand pies, have a cupcake or three, and remember, donations to the couple's favorite charities in lieu of gifts. Information is on the guestbook table."

Wiley lifted his head. "That wasn't in an email you neglected to read."

"I trust Kit to choose a charity or two I support."

"I'm sure Carla told him mine."

Holt nodded but got distracted with kissing everywhere the soft lantern light touched on Wiley's face, and since he was a thorough worker, it took a while. He stopped at Wiley's bow tie and stepped back, too tempted to undo it and Wiley's collar and shirt buttons.

"I suppose we should tear ourselves away to go mingle. Shall we?"

"No" was all Wiley said, and pulled Holt to him for another kiss.

OH, I Do!

Kittens, Holsters, Coyfriends, gather 'round. I'm overjoyed and aflutter for our boys.

Settling in to watch the wedding in my dress pajamas with toast points and Kit-approved rose-gold champagne flute, I didn't expect to cry. But omg, OID family, I bawled. When Holt said his quiet I DO, all deep and without a doubt and his absolute concentration on Wiley, and Wiley just glowing, and then their dance and Holt being the clumsy one and Wiley so confident… I was sent. Well past orbit. I'm talking deep space here.

(I have downloaded that song and it's on heavy rotation as I sing along, and the cats are like, please, have mercy, but there will be none.)

What a splendid dreamy affair it was! Our open thread was hopping and everyone's outfits and cocktail shares made the night so much better. We brought the memes and merriment and snark and devotion—and made the wedding trend on social, worldwide. Boo. Yah.

Also brought? Flowers and decorations and an outpouring of support when word got out the venue was raided—the night before the wedding. What kind of monster, I ask.

The monsters Chief Wilkins already has in custody, that's what.

And, to no one here's surprise, they are no superfans of the show, no sir. (Those would be the outpourers, see above.) Apparently, some punks not from around dear lil Odalia thought filming would provide cover, went on their crime spree, but forgot to cover their faces when they dumped the last of their ill-gotten spoils behind a convenience store not ten miles from town.

Did I just see you perk up? They went to all that criming trouble just to dump everything? Yes, that's right. Chief Wilkins explained they were disgusted to find they hadn't stolen anything of value they could fence. Boxes of flowers and candles and linens—a whole damn cake gone to waste, and that's probably a felony at a wedding? Who could have guessed.

Perhaps calling them monsters is an overstatement. They're like… something slimy and single-celled.

There is a silver lining that makes my heart pitter-pat. It seems Holt's incredibly careful packing of Wiley's village to get them from Wiley's house to the mansion meant they survived the thievery, the rudeness, the dumping. So his cherished grandma's cherished village was safe and safely returned to him.

Let me pause as I go in search of a tissue to get this dust out of my eyes.

I'll update as it proceeds through court. But for now, big yay to Holt for saving the village and the fans who flocked to Odalia and saved the show!

SO. They're married. And Holt is retired. And Kit is moving on.

And we? Are not going anywhere.

Hand to god as the teaser for Kit's new show—*Marry Me, Kit!*—started after the wedding livestream ended I was creating a page and board for it. Kittens, our very own show, with our very own Kit, planning destination weddings in unexpected places that need a little love. Making pop-up stores to sell what the couples get to choose from a permanent feature during filming? Boosting local businesses and economies, all while pulling together the most wonderful weddings ever to be seen?

We don't deserve him. (We do. We really, really do.)

But let's back up to that whole Holt retiring thing. Here's a bit of goss about that, and you know I have the inside scoop lowdown. (Okay, for all this, my source? Our OID attended the wedding as Kit's plus-one contest winner—yes, represent! I knew we could do it. Also, hate you with seething jealousy forever, kiss kiss!) Seems he's in talks with the network to have a show on their streaming platform. Way less formal, way less flash. He and Ben (omg cutie Ben!... omg we're going to need a nickname for cutie Ben) are doing an instructive, pared-down DIY show as they fix up the hardware store. Which, given how Kit talked about it, could take years.

After that? Holt and Ben and Wiley will set up shop. An actual for-real hardware store with Wiley's design studio in the loft. Something about illustrated cards and posters and, pray goodness, T-shirts. If he doesn't design an every-holiday village line, there's no justice in this world. (There is justice in this world, see above.) Something tells me Carla and her cakes will be icing on the whole thing—at least in Ben's heart.

Hmmmmm.

So yes, OID fabs and friends, they might have gotten hitched, said their goodbyes, and taken off for their honeymoon in the actual hills and/or the proverbial hills. But. It's only the beginning for us.

Oh. Yes.

FOR **MORE** OF THE **BEST GAY** ROMANCE

Made in the USA
Las Vegas, NV
19 October 2024